ELYSIUM

ELYSIUM

Robert Edric

Duckworth

For Margaret and Bruce

First published in 1995 by
Gerald Duckworth & Co. Ltd.
The Old Piano Factory
48 Hoxton Square, London N1 6PB
Tel: 0171 729 5986
Fax: 0171 729 0015

A catalogue record for this book is available
from the British Library

ISBN 0 7156 2679 5

Typeset by Ray Davies
Printed in Great Britain by
Redwood Books Limited, Trowbridge

At the last ball at Government House, Hobart Town, there appeared the last male aboriginal inhabitant of Tasmania. Mr Bonwick has this to say: When I went over on a visit to Hobart in 1867, William Lanné had just returned from a whaling voyage. Truganina – known herself by many other names and a good friend to Lanné – had mentioned his being a sailor when talking to me about him. I therefore sought him out. Once I caught sight of him, but he was too intoxicated to talk with. My friend Mr Wooley then gave me one of his excellent photographs of the poor fellow. William Lanné was only thirty-four years of age, and it was considered that his excessive drinking was killing him, shortly to succeed.

Hobart Town Mercury, 14 October 1869

The English said that the prolonged heat on the surface of the Western Ocean sent the sharks in its cold depths into frenzies of feeding and savagery. The same clever fish, they said, that once trailed the transports in expectation of their ballasted corpses. Remember the *Neva*, they said; remember the *Cataraqui*. Imagine those seven hundred women in a wrack of corrupted flesh and greying bones. As though any of them mattered.

But it was also said of the English that they knew everything, and that what they did not know was unknowable. It was an Englishman who discovered why the sky was blue. ('A cannon,' James Fairfax once said, 'in the armoury of our knowledge,' smiling as he spoke.)

Few kept a tally of the early dead – other, that is, than the tallies kept in those hearts where death was always at its most complete and its grief most firmly rooted.

Rooted in the fourteen months since that unseasonable week of the devil beating his wife when no one thought to collect the downfalls that were her tears …

When men sold maps of buried water as though it were treasure …

When tall trees flared and blazed like struck matches.

Later, records were kept. The muster book in the barracks filled its open grave. The journal of the man called Cupid listed and glorified some and covered the faces of others because some were worthy of remembrance and some only of oblivion. In his favour, it can be said of Cupid that he alone, in his office in Government House, transcribed each full name, title and

7

profession with the same cold gaze and solemnity accorded the open gravesite. Life and death were hole and fill to Cupid.

It was an opinion long held that God had created this place using only his left hand. Now they were saying that He had fashioned it spiteful and drunk.

It is the opinion of this newspaper that Mister Lanné is a fraud, and that if any monies are to be spent upon his examination or his preservation, then the same would be better directed elsewhere and to others more worthy of charity in this stricken land. We repeat – A Fraud! Is Science blind?

Hobart Town Daily Courier, 19 April 1863

Something else he remembered long after: he remembered the scientist saying to him, 'And shall we build Jerusalem here, Lanné?' and giving no answer because it was already too late, and because he could not fathom why the question was being asked; the name had changed, but the stink remained.

He remembered too the story of Péron, who believed himself the first into this paradise, and who then discovered a native girl with the name, berth and home town of an English sailor tattooed across her stomach, refusing to allow herself to be sketched by the Frenchman unless this crude claim staked upon her was also exposed.

His name was Lanné; or it was Chappell Joseph the whaler; or it was Matenelager II, misspelt by Robinson, supposed orphan of the Sabine Expedition.

'Am I bound for the Resurrection, do you think?' the scientist had also once asked him, and again he had been unable to answer.

We have no wish to raise the case of Mister Lanné and his Worth and Authenticity any higher, but we firmly believe that for the Sake of History we must not remain silent. We repeat – A Fraud.

Hobart Town Daily Courier, 26 April 1863

1

T HE SUMMONS finally came.
     Two men awaited him.

'You that roll-over bastard Lanné?' the first said.

It had begun as he knew it would begin, as it could only ever begin in that place. He yawned. There was never more than a single invisible track through this particular wilderness.

'I said, You Lanné?' the man repeated. Guttural, prodding, pronouncing it Lanee and drawing out its mocking tail.

'Sir?'

Sometimes it wasn't even a track, sometimes only the unreliable memory of a track.

'William Lanné?'

'Sir?'

The man sat at a desk and looked up at him, a sheet of paper held squarely in both his hands.

'W.C.E.A. Lanné?'

He remained silent; there were limits, and he had spat into that wind before.

'What the initials for?' the other asked him. This second man spoke as though he believed they were something to which Lanné was not entitled, something he might have stolen. Stolen from someone more deserving of them, someone to whom they were better suited, himself.

The first, the man holding the paper, Sergeant Stalker, angry at this interruption, waited to resume.

The corporal – not that the rank counted for anything here –

looked away. His name was Bone. He was in his early twenties but looked much older. His chest and shoulders bore the nipples of untended mosquito bites, and he scratched at these, causing lines of clear liquid to run over his skin before drying in the heat. Bone: boy, youth and man – three generations in that place.

'I asked a question, Lanné.'

Lanné feigned forgetfulness. Some of them liked that: it was all a matter of balances struck, lost and regained.

'The initials.'

'C, E, A,' Bone said.

Stalker slammed his palms on the desk. Its few contents shivered and an empty bottle fell over and rolled its full length, drawing tight the silence in which the three men played their game.

'Charles Edward Albert,' Lanné said.

'Sir,' Bone said.

'Sir.'

Stalker and Bone shared a satisfied glance. The obstacle of their own making had been overcome.

'Very regal,' Bone said.

'What?'

'Kings. They sound like kings.' He shrugged in a half apology. He had taken a step back as the rolling bottle neared the edge of the table.

'They are kings,' Stalker said disbelievingly. 'That's where they get their names.'

'I know that,' Bone said. It embarrassed him to be shouted down in front of this other ignorant bastard.

Stalker traced each name as he repeated them, and Lanné saw by the way his finger moved across the paper that he could not read.

'You read, Lanné?' the sergeant said suddenly.

'Some,' Lanné told him. Yes, no, perhaps.

16

'He's lying,' Bone said, his own illiteracy instantly revealed.

Stalker put down the sheet of paper and smoothed it flat. It was a much-used piece, covered over its entire surface in different hands. Lanné looked down at it in the hope of spotting his name and learning something these other two were unable to tell him. But the scrawl was illegible. In places it was thick and clumsy; in others so minute that it looked like fallen hairs. Some messages had run out of space and had meandered like flood streams in search of new courses.

'How much do you read?' Stalker said.

'Not much.' A good foundation stone for a column of lies.

'This much?' Stalker held out the sheet for Lanné to see more clearly.

'None of that, sir,' Lanné said. The 'sir' was a mistake and both he and Stalker knew it. With men like Lanné it concealed too much. Others used it like a snake uses its tongue, a test before commitment. Most intended it as a suggestion of disarming bewilderment – a request for guidance as might be sought by an idiot or a child.

Neither man spoke.

The previous evening, Lanné had read the final chapter of 'The Old Curiosity Shop' to Eumarah, Ruby and Pearl, the book borrowed from the Bethel library. He remembered the closing words and silently repeated them to himself. *Such are the changes that a few years bring about, and so do things pass away, like a tale that is told.* A quartet of angels, one playing a harp, bearing the small child up into Heaven. Eumarah, Ruby and Pearl were all firm believers in Heaven, and he had held up the book for them to look at the illustration through their tears. He had almost cried himself, but not for the dead child.

'He can't read sod all,' Bone said triumphantly. Stalker remained unconvinced.

Bone decided to press home his advantage. 'Go on, read that first line, read what it says, I want to hear.'

Stalker pushed the paper closer to him. 'Known about this all along, haven't we, Billy?' he said, unwilling to prolong the charade. He sat back in his seat and wiped the sweat from his face.

'What? About what? What is it?' Bone said, but Stalker ignored him.

It pleased Lanné to see one man whet his humour on the other's ignorance. 'Knew a couple of days ago,' he said.

'That wild mob come in?' Stalker said.

Lanné nodded.

In truth, Lanné felt some sympathy for the two men. He filled an hour of their otherwise empty day and soon the thickening heat would get to them through their flimsy walls. And it would come down through the roof at them and up through the earth of the floor at them.

'Knows what?' Bone said.

Stalker slid the sheet of paper into the desk's only drawer, his frustration now eased by amusement.

Lanné closed his eyes as the two men continued to quiz him, shepherding his hangover towards noon, testing its boundaries and direction. He had known for two days that he would be summoned, but there had been nothing he could do to prepare himself.

He looked past them through the small window to the compound beyond, where everything remained distorted in the powdery haze: a rack of skins pegged out to cure, and beside them, strung along a frame, an abacus of skulls. He could hear the voices of small children chanting from a book of Scripture.

'Nice suit,' Bone said unexpectedly, drawing him back to them. The corporal tested the material of the lapel and brushed dust from Lanné's shoulders.

'Belongs to Walter George Augustus,' Lanné said. Everything, one way or another, belonged to Walter George Augustus.

'Town ought to be called after the fat black bastard,' Bone said.

Lanné nodded in agreement.

Walter George Augustus would be somewhere close by, probably in the shade of the guardroom, or hidden with his eye on the entrance, anxious to reclaim his jacket and waistcoat and trousers, his shirt and his shoes. And in return for the loan Lanné would be required to give a full account of what had taken place. The bounds of Walter George Augustus' generosity were very clearly defined.

'Come all the way from England,' Stalker said. He was referring to the scientist.

'Didn't know.' It was his first entirely honest answer.

'Great honour, Billy.'

The greatest. The man was still on his way from Flinders in the Government packet. It would be another week before he arrived, ten days if Bonaparte's predictions were to be believed.

'Honour? What honour? For him?' Bone stopped running his fingers over Lanné's shoulders.

'Big man, our Billy here,' Stalker said. 'Ought really to start calling him William.'

'Not me,' Bone said.

'The last of the few.'

'Few what?'

'After you, Billy,' Stalker said, ignoring Bone. 'After you ...' He smiled and drew a finger across the grey stubble of his throat.

Bone, realizing what was being said, copied with the blade of his own finger. But half-way through the gesture, his face still close to Lanné's, he stopped. His eyes grew large, as though, despite staring hard into Lanné's own, he was trying to identify something impossibly distant.

'The last,' Stalker said. 'Something of an honour, really. All the way from England.'

'Something to tell your –' Bone began.

Lanné stopped listening. King Billy, hammer of all Bone's ancestors.

Above him a galaxy of torpid flies rolled in countless orbits from one end of the low ceiling to the other and back again.

He left an hour later and walked out into the compound, aware that somewhere Walter George Augustus would be watching him. Like the Eye of God he would be watching him. He pulled out a starched handkerchief and wiped his brow, blinded by its sudden whiteness as he signalled his indifference to the man.

He was drawn to the chanting voices and came to where a preacher conducted a group of Mission strays. They faltered at Lanné's approach and the man regained their rhythm with his cane on their heads.

Bonaparte and his mob had run from Falmouth with the news. Their scarified skin and painted nakedness disgusted Walter George Augustus and he ordered Mary Ann from the room so that this barbaric intrusion would not distress her.

It was his opinion that Bonaparte had come from Falmouth via every bar still open to him, and that he had waited on the outskirts of the town until he was sober enough to present himself, running only the final few yards before arriving so dramatically at Eumarah's.

Eumarah washed the ash and dirt from his limbs. She gave him a clean yellow cloth to fasten round his waist. Afterwards he was allowed on to the bleached sagging boards of the veranda, where he squatted sullen and silent for an hour, withholding the news he was so desperate to impart.

'He can't speak,' Walter George Augustus said, as though this confirmed everything he had said about the savage.

Only Mary Ann, who had by then been allowed to return,

was vigorous in support of her husband. 'Look at him, he's like a wild creature,' she said.

'So true,' Walter George Augustus said. 'But more than that. He is a reminder to us all of what we all once were, and what –'

'And what we all might yet become if we are not careful in maintaining … in maintaining …' Mary Ann faltered. Normally she made conversation like a woman carelessly emptying her pockets.

Walter George Augustus smiled proudly and finished the sentence for her.

The rest of the mob stood back in the shade of the trees, barely visible amid the stipple of shadow and light.

Ruby and Pearl stood with their chins up and their eyes closed, and by this simple gesture denied their presence.

Lanné liked Bonaparte. They were distant cousins. He liked him for the man he had remained, and he knew that were it not for Bonaparte's wilder excesses, they would all search for some lost part of themselves in him. Except Walter George Augustus and Mary Ann, who sought in others only what they might yet become. To Lanné, Walter George Augustus and his wife were the two pillars of an unfinished temple upon whose heads rested the marble portico announcing that here was Civilization, here were all things Good, Proper, Honest and Decent.

Seeing that they were unlikely to be given any drink, some of the mob became restless and several came out into the open and called for Bonaparte to return to them.

'The bars must be open,' Mary Ann said.

Bonaparte rose and waved the distant men into silence.

'Complete waste of time,' he said to Lanné. 'You knew already.'

Lanné did, but was not certain how he knew.

'Why does he have to talk in such ridiculous riddles?' Mary Ann asked her husband.

To his credit, Walter George Augustus said nothing.

21

Bonaparte ran a hand over his tight stomach. He picked up his stick and his waddy. 'We were going anyway,' he said.

It was Bonaparte who, upon being offered a sixpenny bounty by the Old Governor's wife for every snakeskin handed over, immediately went in search of every nest he knew of and hatched out the hundreds of eggs he collected in a secret cache of molasses barrels. And when this supply was exhausted, and the Governor's wife had still not realized what was happening, it was Bonaparte and his mob who had stripped every snakeskin tree in Kent County of its bark, cut this into appropriate lengths and then branded eyes into each piece. It was Bonaparte who retrieved the hastily-buried bodies of their dead and took them away into the bush for the painting and the reed-wrapping they cried out for.

Lanné wished that *he* was the last pure-breed. The burden would have been nothing on his shoulders.

Bonaparte left the veranda and beckoned Lanné to follow him.

'No whispering,' Mary Ann shouted, tugging at her husband's sleeve for him to intervene.

'Ask the three old birds,' Bonaparte told Lanné. He indicated Eumarah, Ruby and Pearl, all of whom stood in their faded print dresses with their arms folded across their flat chests. 'Ever occur to you that the world is filling up with stupid questions?' he said. He tapped Lanné's arm with the tip of his stick, said, 'You're a dead man, Billy Lanné,' and burst into laughter. Then he went to join the others, who were already drifting away. As he went he unfastened the square of yellow cloth and laid it carefully on the ground.

Lanné resisted the urge to follow him. He resisted too the urge to call out after him, 'You, too, Bonaparte, you're a dead man, too.'

The plan to rid the island of its snakes had ended with the departure of the Old Governor. Afterwards the man had led two shiploads of brave explorers into a lost, icy grave. A photograph of his wife, a gift upon her departure, looked down on everyone invited into Mary Ann's parlour.

The others left the veranda and went indoors.

The look in Walter George Augustus' eyes as Lanné came back to him said, 'Why you and not me? Where is the justice in this world?'

Old and dry now, Eumarah had once been a great beauty. Eumarah, variously spelt, cast aside, mother and sister to Andromanche, Margaret, Teelapana and Crank Poll. And possessor of, among others, Violet and Teddeburic, otherwise Princess Clara. She confessed to Lanné to feeling lost as she grew older.

'And shrinking,' she said to him as they sat together. She pulled at the slack of the dress into which she could have fitted twice. Given to her by the Ladies of the Scotch Mission, handdown and shapeless, its battleground of holes and tears repaired with no regard for the colour or pattern beneath.

When Lanné had first arrived here, twenty years ago, not knowing where he was or where he had come from, and woken only by the fall when the carter kicked a boy from his cart, it was Eumarah who had helped him to his feet. Away from the wheels and into this house of old women, where she told him he could stay, and where, his wanderings and absences apart, he had lived ever since. She was mother to him. Ruby and Pearl, the same age as Eumarah, he looked on as benevolent aunts. Ruby and Pearl – two of a string of counterfeit jewels and barely-precious stones from which to choose. With other missions it was gardens of flowers – beds of Lilies and Roses and Daisies to be plucked and scattered and grown again.

Eumarah confessed to him that she did not regret the loss of her beauty. Not since Walter George Augustus had pointed out

23

to her that as a young woman she had behaved little better than a Judas.

Lanné was with her when he had said it, ten years ago, striking the air between them with the rolled journal in which some small part of her distant history was recounted. He called her a disgrace, and because even then she had been an old woman and had refused to defend herself, Lanné had grabbed the journal from him, jabbed him in the stomach with it and then punched him in the face. There had been an anger in him in those days which no longer existed. Blood trickled from Walter George Augustus' nose and mouth. No one had hit him like that since he was a small child. Lanné regretted it and helped him to a seat. He doused a cloth in water and gave it to him to hold against his lips. Then he told him to apologize to Eumarah for what he'd said. Walter George Augustus mumbled through his pain and the cloth.

The journal lay on the ground beside Eumarah, slowly uncurling, as though it were some living thing intent on surprise.

When she was a young woman Eumarah had gone with the militia to help in their gathering and resettlement programmes. She had enticed people out of their hiding places with promises of good treatment and respect. Whole families had followed her out of the darkness into the light, whole tribes. She had travelled from Robbin to Gun Carriage, Weymouth to Marlborough. There had been many love matches. She spoke several languages.

All this lasted for ten years, and everything that happened in that time she kept locked inside her.

It was true what Walter George Augustus said. Her beauty had been used as the bait in a trap. All she ever told Lanné was that the young officer who had promised to marry her and take her with him to the mainland when she reached twenty-one came to her on the eve of his departure, slept with her, told her he was leaving without her, and then laughed at her and spat in

24

her face. There had been a struggle and he had broken the two small fingers of her left hand. These had never properly healed, and remained rigid. Much later she refused the Old Governor's offer to have his surgeon attend to them so that she might at least have some small degree of control over them. She chose them as the first of her punishments and reminders.

When the bleeding stopped and he was able to speak without wincing, Walter George Augustus apologized again.

Lanné learned afterwards that it was not he who had discovered the reference to Eumarah's past, but another member of the Town Council, a newly-arrived Englishman, who had rolled up the journal and jabbed it into Walter George Augustus' chest just as he had then done with Eumarah.

'Don't tell Mary Ann about any of this,' he told them, this being the price of his apology.

He and Mary Ann had not been long married and he was still educating her. They had not then moved into the house he was having built away from the settlement and close to the Courts; she had not yet finished mourning the loss of her own family; and the newly-weds had yet to discover that their life together was to remain childless.

Lanné picked up the journal and gave it back to him, and in an act of conciliation Walter George Augustus tore it in half and then half again and threw the pieces towards the open door.

Still Eumarah sat with her head bowed and said nothing.

Understanding Walter George Augustus' reverence for all things printed, Lanné knew that he could not make his apology any more forcefully. The two men reached an understanding on that day and ever afterwards there had remained a distance between them.

Eventually Eumarah said that she did not blame him. There was nothing Walter George Augustus could tell her, or of which he could accuse her, that she had not herself already fought – and failed – to come to peace with. It was why, ten years ago, she had renounced all her old names and the title princess. It was why she had disappeared for three months and come back looking like she did. Her beauty died, and her faith and belief in it. Just as those terrified figures stumbling out of their caves had died.

The Ladies of the Scotch called her Mary, and every time she heard it she corrected them. But they treated her denials as though they were soft harmless balls to be batted back at her.

That occurrence long ago had ended with the arrival of Ruby and Pearl. Lanné gathered up the pieces of the journal and Eumarah told them that a child had run past the open doorway and thrown them in. Such were the ways, it then occurred to Lanné, that they denied themselves. And in their acts of denial, so they all set themselves adrift.

And so they started calling him King Billy. Homesteaders and old ticket-of-leavers. Even their women and bedwarmers. The quartermasters and barracks men. His every entrance became the occasion for a joke. He played along with them. He was invited into bars where previously he had only been served at the hatch. Men put their arms around his shoulders. Women and children stopped their gossip and play in the street to watch him pass. He received invitations from two of the town photographers to pose free of charge in their studios. He received requests from clerks and land agents to be pictured alongside them. One of the barmen put up a sign above his barrels: As Frequented By Royalty. Except 'Frequented' was misspelt and later changed for 'Drunk'.

Windless oceans. Ten days in a calm of waiting. Boundless horizons lost only to the inability of an imagination spent peering through white trees and into sunless holes. A ship, then no ship. The Tasman Company shipping agents listed the vessel, the *Eudora*, but gave no passenger list.

Lanné dreamed one night that he was the victim of a hoax, and woke no less certain that this was not what had happened. Only Eumarah convinced him that he had been told the truth.

Ruby and Pearl enjoyed his uncertain celebrity far more than he ever could, and Eumarah's glance warned him against disabusing them.

'So there is no way forward,' she said when he told her all that had passed between himself and the two soldiers. There was an essential truth in her words, one that would not be confused by whatever else he might want to hear or believe. He felt like a man awaiting a judgement. He felt like an innocent man about to be found unjustly guilty of some heinous crime.

'No way forward, no way back,' Ruby said. Often she and Pearl held long, convoluted conversations where their sole purpose was to elaborate upon something Eumarah had already said. They moved in circles, weaving and binding, pleased with themselves whenever the original point was later touched upon, delirious with achievement on the rare occasions when something of equal significance was reached. But usually they lost their subjects in tangles of misunderstanding. Mary Ann told them they sounded like the mina birds kept by the Governor.

Eumarah was tolerant of them and had long since learned to conserve her own vital energies at the centre of their storms. They were left arm and right arm to her, and she would feel their loss even more keenly. When Lanné was drunk, one or other of the women made sure he was carried home. When he failed to appear for casual work or other appointments they brushed over his tracks with excuses. And when he was away with the Rangers or on a whaling trip they prayed twice a day for his safe deliverance.

Eumarah alone entered with him into the limbo of waiting.

27

She knew as well as he did that there were others, that he was not what they said he was: others left wild, born and living and dead unseen and uncounted. But she knew too that he could not now refute what they told him and what they wanted to believe.

'They draw their lines with you and me,' she told him. 'With you and me they close their book.'

Later she told him that planning any evasion would be as useless as plotting the collision courses of dying stars in the night sky.

The word 'destiny' was used – a stake to which he might yet be tied, expectation piled like brushwood at his feet.

2

J AMES ADOLARIUS Loftus Fairfax. A man who wore his past as though it were a band of medals across his chest, easy reminders of times, places and achievements. He was twenty-four years and eight days old. His birthday had fallen two days into the Bass Strait. He did not mark the occasion. It embarrassed him that the only person on the vessel younger than himself was a twelve-year-old boy. He did not miss the celebration, it did not matter to him. What mattered to him was the substance of fact and figures. The substance of his name. The substance of his work yet to be performed. The only miracles he believed in were the miracles of Science. It had been his father's boast that his only son, by the age of nine, had read every book in his large library and was able to discuss their contents with anyone prompted to put him to the test.

James Fairfax's first miracle had come during his attendance of a lecture at the Royal Academy for Science, during which electricity had been used to bring back to the semblance of life a severed human hand. He bore with him still the flexing and the curling of those drained white fingers and thumb, the sudden filling out of slack muscle and flesh. His wonder – this is what mattered to him.

He was born in Kensington. His father was a Chancery lawyer, blinded in a shooting accident in Scotland when his son was eight years old. His mother died when he was young. He could not remember a time when he had felt any true affection for her. His only profit was the sympathy of others.

He was educated at Cholmeley Grammar School in Highgate, and then at Oxford.

Then, when James Fairfax was nineteen, the world and all its certainties shifted on its axis. A succession of defeats ruined his father and he watched his inheritance fall from seventy thousand pounds to less than eight hundred, as a consequence of which he left for Australia to live with his uncle, the grazier and judge, James Langton Fairfax, at Ballarat, a man renowned for dipping his native herders along with his shorn sheep.

James Fairfax's first task there was to help the old man translate the works of Balzac so that he might repeat the stories to his station hands. A translation was afterwards published, for which James Fairfax received neither payment nor acknowledgment. He could not contain his bitterness at this and so, a year after his arrival, he left Ballarat and worked as a clerk and a journalist in Sydney.

His interest in scientific pursuits never faded. He became involved in the study of the mainland natives, was appointed a member of the Protection League, and afterwards given the job of editing its journal, to which he also contributed. For two years he took camphor treatments to safeguard himself against lascivious thoughts and dreams.

At sea, with land in sight neither ahead nor astern, James Fairfax began to calculate how much of what was behind him he might now discard once his name and reputation were established anew. His blind father had taken his own life while his son was at Ballarat, and so that part of him, the old man's memories glowing with paternal fondness, was already lost. The judge too was marching into the palatial oblivion of insanity. It all fell and drifted out of sight behind him like jettisoned waste. And as with his dead mother, he felt no real loss in any of these severed attachments.

I am a scientist, he would tell people. It impressed. It mystified. His purpose was signalled long in advance of his involvement. I am here to do this. I am here to do this. There was a logical progression by which the correct results would be achieved. Where other men saw debased savages, better caged or dead than alive, James Fairfax saw only his own impressive name printed in full, bold and impressive across a clean white beginning. He was – and he would admit this to no one but himself – little different from one of those ballast-hungry sharks, alert and ever searching, and with only his appetites to guide and sustain him.

For the four calm days of the open crossing he was violently sick. It was an inauspicious start to his new self.

Then six further days with land in sight. The tug of a wrecking swell, but nothing more. Sickness and fear. He lost a stone in those ten days. He grew pale. He bruised his brow and cheek when a loose block swung against him as he was vomiting over the side one morning.

And then the calm of Storm Bay. Two days of recovery and preparation.

Alone in his cabin, James Fairfax stared hard into the lifeless eyes of his fiancée, pressed her cold glass to his lips and swore his name and his success to her.

This was his arrival.

'You can't be the last.'

Lanné was on his way back from the camp. The man rose from a ditch with a billhook held above him. All around him the crops in his fields were dead.

'Pissed on better looking specimens than you down on the quay when they were gathering up for Swan.' The memory amused him. He spat heavily at Lanné's feet. He was clearing a channel where once water had flowed from the river on to his land. Lanné knew him, but only by sight.

'You're one of that civilized mob. You're not civilized, none of you. That what you think you are?'

31

Everything in the small clearing behind the man was dead. Even the trees which waited to close in on his ramshackle home looked lifeless. A man could swing an axe into one of those trunks and every last leaf from every branch would shower him. In the years of reliable rain, wild corn and barley had seethed to the horizon.

'I asked you a question.'

'Long time without rain,' Lanné said. He could not gauge what the man expected of him.

'Forget the rain. You think rain's going to bring all this back to life? It's dead. Everything's dead. My wife lost a baby on account of the rain.'

Lanné looked closer at his sallow skin, at the yellowing of his cheeks and forehead.

Then a movement at the edge of the withered crops caught his attention. Another man rose from where he'd been squatting. Black and skeletal. At first Lanné thought he was wearing a large hat, but as the man approached he saw that this was his hair – uncut and matted and stiff with grease and ash so that it stuck out in all directions. A male Medusa. Tatters of cloth and bead-strung twine were fastened in it.

The man in the ditch turned. 'He's mine. He's an idle black bastard. You all are.'

Lanné wondered what there was for the hired hand to do.

He approached, stopping twenty feet behind his employer, as though this were some arrangement they had made at his hiring.

'Get back to work.'

But the man stood and watched them. It surprised Lanné that he had not seen him before.

'See.'

'We're all idle black bastards,' Lanné said.

The man swung his billhook, throwing up dusty clods. His labour was useless momentum, anything but idleness.

32

'No rain, no babies. I knocked her up good and full, and it grew in her just like all the others, and then half a year there's no rain and it dies, still inside her, three weeks before she's due.' He slashed suddenly at the dry grass at Lanné's feet. 'Where's the bloody justice in that? And now all this.' He continued slashing as he spoke.

Only once before had Lanné seen frustration kill a man, but he had only understood this long afterwards, and by then his father's bones had been taken away.

The drains on a thousand other homesteads had silted up, just as fat meat seized on the bone.

'You a bloody savage, too?' the man said.

'Probably,' Lanné told him.

In the field, the third man turned and walked away into the trees. He paused only once, and then to turn and gaze directly at Lanné before crossing into the undergrowth. At that distance his head looked solid and full, an unsupportable weight on the pole of his spine.

'You want to work here?'

Lanné shook his head.

'I got grown daughters been messed with by your mob. Look here.' He took something from his pocket, but kept whatever it was hidden in his palm, laughed at it and then pushed it back before Lanné was able to see it. He could only guess. Even the Governor had his collection of confiscated tobacco stoppers.

The man's energy came and went in manic starts.

'Why they never sent you off to one of the camps?'

They did. 'Don't know.'

'Learnt the language, I suppose.'

Lanné looked beyond him, to the woman who had just then appeared in the doorway of their decrepit home. She stood with a small child clutched to her chest. Several others appeared beside her. Lanné could only imagine what happened in that dark place, what terrors were born of her husband's persecution. The man saw where he was looking but did not himself turn to acknowledge her.

'Died right inside her. Pulled the carcass out myself. She healed up. Didn't think she would, but she did. Never since, never again.' He started to slaver.

A line of soldiers marched towards them in their desultory fashion and Lanné stood back to let them pass. When they had gone he looked across to the ditch and saw that the man had left it and was running back towards his wife and children, shouting and waving his hook. The woman shut the door on him long before he arrived.

Walter George Augustus intercepted the Governor's message and delivered it to Lanné where he slept at the quarry. He had been working there for two days, but now the blasting had ended.

Walter George Augustus pulled him to his feet from his granite bed.

'Naturally, I am to accompany you.'

Before Lanné was fully aware of what was happening, Walter George Augustus was behind him and pushing him in the direction of the town.

They stopped at a rendezvous with Mary Ann and she handed over the clothes to make Lanné presentable.

'I think he'd rather see me naked,' Lanné said. Mary Ann slapped his cheek. It was 110 degrees. They dismissed all his arguments. Mary Ann slapped him again. She fastened a tie and pulled it tight to his throat. Children gathered around them until scattered by Walter George Augustus. Lanné naked might have been fair bait for their taunts and stones; Lanné in his shirt, jacket and trousers was not. Mary Ann arranged a handkerchief in Lanné's pocket and warned him against using it. A satisfied smile crossed her fat wet face as she stepped back to look at him, a proud mother looking at her Academy son perhaps, and for a moment Lanné braced himself against the kiss which never came.

Walter George Augustus held him by the arm and led him away.

'Like a lamb to the slaughter in the slaughterhouse of Christian enlightenment,' Lanné said aloud to his audience. The children cheered him.

At Government House, Walter George Augustus told him to wait while he went to inform Cupid of their arrival.

'Sit down. Sit with your back straight and with your arms by your side. Keep both feet on the ground, together, facing forward. Hold your hat in your lap and don't whistle. Speak to no one unless spoken to first.'

'No hat,' Lanné said.

'What?'

'No hat.' Lanné patted his bare head.

'But I gave her one to give you. I gave her one. I distinctly told her. I did, I gave her one.'

'Perhaps she forgot,' Lanné suggested. These were the cracks that let in the light.

Walter George Augustus came back to him and gave him his own bowler.

'Perhaps it blew off and I never noticed,' Lanné said.

Walter George Augustus stared at him for a moment. 'I distinctly remember telling her.'

They were interrupted by the appearance of Cupid, who emerged from the Governor's office, passed through his own small antechamber and came out into the waiting room. He carried a large ledger, upon which was balanced a sheaf of papers. He was rarely seen without that ledger, or some other like it. He carried it the way judges wore their wigs and the way officers carried their canes. He carried it as though he might have written everything in it, and he caressed its leather covers as though it contained the wisdom or the secrets of the world.

'Ah, Mr Lanné,' he said. He was a small, vain, precise man. One of the few who ever made a point of pronouncing Lanné's name correctly. 'And Walter George Augustus,' he added with a sigh. He encountered the man almost daily on some petty business or other. 'Excellent news on the ship.'

'Excellent,' Walter George Augustus said, masking his ignorance.

Lanné had no idea of the whereabouts of the vessel, of the arrow of his future aimed directly at him. And for the first time he began to wonder about the appearance and the nature of the man on his way to see him. It worried him that it might be a man with a mission to fulfil. And he speculated too on which of them had the most to gain from the encounter. He was not yet certain of the William Lanné he would present.

'I believe the summons was for Mr Lanné alone,' Cupid said.

'He insisted I accompany him. His interests deserve the fullest protection.' Walter George Augustus looked enviously at the book as he spoke. He would practise carrying around the heaviest of his own volumes in the privacy of his home. Perhaps the one he balanced on Mary Ann's head during his instruction on deportment.

Cupid was not prepared to argue.

A bell rang on the wall beside his desk.

'Go through,' he said. 'I would accompany you, take notes, but my duties elsewhere are of rather greater importance.' He left them and walked briskly out into the light of the garden.

Three nights earlier he had approached Lanné in the quarry drinkhouse and given him the card of one of the town photographers. 'You and I?' he had said.

The Governor rose to meet them and to shake hands. 'Something of an honour,' he said, but without any conviction. 'A celebrity in our midst. Royalty, I believe. A real pleasure.' He spoke as though he were seeing Lanné for the first time. The last time he had spoken to him was to sentence him to ten days in the Darling Street gaol for drunkenness. He had forgotten.

'Say "Thank you, sir",' Walter George Augustus hissed in Lanné's ear.

Lanné said it. He looked quickly round the over-filled room, its every space, floor and wall, crowded with mementoes of a better life elsewhere, with furniture, prints and books. An open window looked out on to a dead lawn and the river beyond.

'You do understand the nature of Mr Fairfax's visit, I assume,' the Governor said.

Fairfax.

Lanné nodded, said, 'Sir.'

Walter George Augustus said, 'I think I ought to make a note of the name, sir. Unless, of course, you object.' He took out a small notebook, to which a pencil was attached, licked its tip and started to write. 'Is that Doctor Fairfax? Professor?'

The Governor did not know. Nor did he search the papers on his desk for an answer.

'A purely scientific inquiry. An investigation into the purely physiological aspects of ... of ... well, of *you*, Lanné.'

'Physiological,' Walter George Augustus repeated.

'Nothing will be conducted against your will. You have my assurance on that. My absolute assurance.'

'Conducted?' Walter George Augustus said. 'Experiments?' He became keener.

Lanné stepped to one side so that the two men might continue their discussion without the inconvenience of his own contribution. And it was only as he stood and wished himself invisible, or at least asleep back in the quarry, that he realized how fully he had already acquiesced in what was happening to him. He stared up at the slowly turning fan, its blades quivering as they spun.

'The Protection Committee have of course been informed of

Mr Fairfax's intentions. We can allow no repetition of past incidents, however accidental.' The Governor cleared his throat. A large brass and marble clock struck four, and upon Walter George Augustus turning to acknowledge it, the Governor led him towards it and pointed out its features to him.

They meant Burke's Hut, thought Lanné. Risdon Cove. The drunkard Moore seeing double and shouting Fire! And Mountgarret's bones on the *Ocean* headed for Sydney. They meant the North Esk drownings and the Fingal corral. They meant the King River discovery and the shaming Belvoir pits between Surrey and Magog.

The clock was a present from the Governor's wife upon his appointment to that place. She was twenty-four years his junior and lived for weeks on end without leaving their home. Her footsteps on the upper floor were listened to in sudden, fearful silences below. She had been raised in India, where her father had served, Delhi and Lucknow, and she had expected the same life here.

'And you see the regulators,' the Governor said to Walter George Augustus, both of them crouched over the clock. 'Solid gold. Welsh gold.'

'Welsh,' Walter George Augustus said. 'The best, in my opinion.'

The Governor then returned to Lanné. 'Delighted we could put your mind at rest,' he said. He and Walter George Augustus had become co-conspirators. It was now Walter George Augustus' duty to take Lanné away.

On the street outside they encountered Cupid again, still with his ledger, but this time with a packet of meat balanced on it. He tried unsuccessfully to hide from them and then walked quickly away to a side entrance.

'What experiments?' Lanné said.

Walter George Augustus ignored him, snatching back his bowler so that he might raise it to any passing acquaintance.

When she heard the word experiment, Eumarah wailed, slapping her sides with her palms. Ruby and Pearl copied her.

Alarmed by this show of pity for him – made worse for coming from three old women over twice his age – Lanné left them and went in search of Bonaparte.

He found him in the bed of the Derwent, scooping up mud and smearing himself, plastering it beneath his arms and over his genitals, where it baked dry on him as fast as he spread it.

At first Lanné thought he was alone, but then he saw the two others. He recognized both from the days he and Bonaparte had worked together in the greenstone mines at Cox Creek.

One was a man called Mackamee, rechristened Washington. As boys he and Lanné had worked together as water carriers. He rose from where he lay and came to greet Lanné.

The other was a man known as Albino Billy. He claimed he was descended from the chiefs of the Big River mob, and that Calamaroweyne, the murderer of Captain Thomas, was his grandfather. Few believed him. He denied all his white blood. His few brown teeth had been filed to points. When he smiled it was with the raw wet menace of a wild dog. Lanné was wary of him. He wished there was some way of warning Bonaparte of the man's recklessness without making him sound even more appealing. Five years ago Albino Billy had been implicated in the murder of a woman and her two children in Burgess. The three settlers had been dead a month before being discovered by the husband and father on his return from the sea. His pale flesh looked as though it was dusted with flour. There was no colour in his eyes, and on his thigh there was a raised scar where a bullet had taken a piece out of him. This had never properly healed and was now a lump the size of a man's fist and looked like the bark of a tree grown over a severed branch. Albino Billy was one of God's black jokes.

39

'You hear about my father?' Bonaparte said as Lanné sat beside him.

'No. What?'

'Killed on Flinders.'

'But that was twelve years ago.'

'So what?'

Lanné was accustomed to these games, these back and forth matches where the distinction between accuser and accused was always lost. He knew what came next.

'Hear about your own father?' Bonaparte said.

'I heard.'

A long silence followed.

'You ought to come with us,' Bonaparte said eventually. 'Join us.'

Neither Washington nor Albino Billy showed any enthusiasm for the suggestion.

'Why? You leaving?' Lanné spread some of the remaining mud over the soles of his feet. The river was almost dry. Even the damp flower of its source was said to be failing.

'Might be. Might stay and watch you measured up, chopped into pieces and pickled.'

Albino Billy laughed.

'Can't happen,' Lanné said. 'I'm royalty.'

This time all four men laughed.

'They're still telling us that we're cannibals up on Circular Head,' Washington said. 'Them. Telling us.'

It occurred to Lanné to ask him if he remembered the old name for the place. He'd heard the stories. It was a wild place and they were a desperate tribe.

It was difficult for him to talk to Bonaparte with these others present.

'See that?' Bonaparte said, clasping both hands to his full stomach. 'We found a sheep lost its way. Asked it to join us for a feast.'

'And presumably you buried the remains.'

'And pissed on the fire.'

Lanné wondered why, if Bonaparte insisted on living so dangerously, of making a point of letting others know what he was doing, why he did it so close to the town and the barracks. Half the militia on the island was quartered less than an hour away. A rifle shot could be heard twenty miles in that dry air.

'*Are* you leaving?' Lanné repeated, knowing that this was unlikely, that Bonaparte would at least want to see the scientist now that he was so close.

If it hadn't been for Eumarah and the others, Lanné believed he might have accepted Bonaparte's offer. But now that road was blocked to him. A life of frayed ends was being woven together, pulled tight and ready for binding. Just as an old rope was salvaged and made useful again.

'You think you have to live up to something?' Bonaparte asked him.

Lanné shrugged.

'*Their* expectations?'

'Should have got some white in you like us,' Washington said, moving out of reach of the albino as he spoke. 'Should have had your grandmother turned lubra at twelve then none of this would be happening to you.'

'Never knew her,' Lanné said.

'Not the point. Never knew mine, but whatever she had in her –' Washington rubbed his crotch '– I still got in me.'

Like Lanné, the others did not know how to respond to this, and they waited for Washington's own cold laughter before grinning themselves.

'You'd better go,' Bonaparte told him. 'Let your old women deal with it.'

'Wouldn't surprise me if they tried to mate you with some Mainland pure-breed,' the albino said. 'One of them gins with yeller hair.'

Their laughter followed Lanné back up the crumbling bank and into the bush.

There was a dream Lanné inhabited. It was of a time before his birth. Or so he assumed. Because although it was a place with which he was familiar, there was also something about it wholly unfamiliar. A richness and a peacefulness which no longer existed. It was a dreamlike place, and his existence within it was dreamlike. And when he walked out of it, and afterwards woke from it, he was left with an inexplicable longing, as though there were a taste of something sweet on his tongue inside an empty mouth.

Afterwards, when he tried to explain this to Eumarah, she told him to stop, that he would only confuse and disappoint himself by his inability to do so. She said it was something they had all tasted. And when he asked her what it meant, she said that it meant nothing. This surprised him. He knew how tightly she clung to her own dreams. She, Ruby and Pearl discussed them endlessly. And on many occasions the three of them professed to have inhabited identical dreams at the same time – on occasion all three waking from them in the same instant. He knew that these shared dreams were invested with a significance more potent and satisfying than much of what they shared together in the dull routine of their waking lives.

He insisted on describing for her what he had seen and what he had done in his dream.

'This is what used to set them off wandering,' she told him, still unwilling to encourage him.

Each time she spoke, Lanné noticed, she flicked her eyes away from him. She was keeping something from him, and it was not like her.

'People like Bonaparte, you mean?' It was the simplest answer, the one he most wanted to hear.

'And others.'

He wondered if she was thinking of her own seven long-dead brothers.

'Are they looking for something? Are they looking for whatever place it is they see in their dreams?'

She shook her head.

Six months ago he would have laughed disparagingly at all this talk of dreams. It was early afternoon; six months ago he would have been crawling drunk.

They left her home and walked together along the road leading from the camp to the town. Alongside them the old quays rotted and melted into the river. The deepwater channel had shifted from one bank to the other. Sandbanks lay exposed like muscles in flesh.

'Time was it didn't matter to worry about the distinction,' she said. 'Dreaming, waking, it didn't matter.'

'And now it does?' He was not prepared for where this might lead him. His life had been spent avoiding these undefinable responsibilities.

'I don't know what you want me to say. I don't know what to tell you.' She looked at him squarely for the first time. This woman who would sit silently for six hours pounding seed. This woman who would unpick the wool of a shirt and bemoan the loss of a wasted inch. Who would disappear for days on end and then return as unexpectedly as she had gone, saying nothing to anyone, as though she had just woken from a short nap.

It was beyond Lanné to ask her if she thought his dream of this perfect place and his own place within it had any connection with what was about to happen to him.

They stopped beside an old man asleep on the road. From a distance Lanné thought him to be a branch fallen from a logger's wagon. Only as they drew closer did he see the man's hands clasped between his thighs, his naked buttocks presented to them. He lay face down and snored loudly, blowing up small eddies of dust at every breath.

Eumarah bent down and gently turned the old man's sleeping head so that his nose and lips were not pressed so firmly into the ground.

'You know him?' Lanné asked her.

Eumarah shook her head, but too quickly for him to believe her.

There were to be more dreams, he understood that. 'They live in you,' Eumarah was to tell him later, much later, when the time came for him to save himself. 'They live in you just as you live in them.'

She moved ahead of him, seeming almost to glide along the dusty road.

3

'CAN YOU imagine a fate more terrible than the inability to accept change, Mr Lanné?'

Lanné sat at the desk where, until a moment earlier, James Fairfax had been sitting facing him. Now the scientist stood behind him, his hands on Lanné's shoulders.

'Answer him,' Bone said.

The corporal and the sergeant sat on a bench at the side of the room. It was the same room in which Lanné had seen the two men fifteen days earlier.

'No, no, Mr Lanné, please. The question was purely hypothetical,' James Fairfax said, annoyed by the intrusion. He would have preferred to meet Lanné alone. He was only here, in this unsuitable room, because he had not understood the layout of the camp and the living quarters and had accepted the Governor's first offer. It was the Governor too who had insisted that he be accompanied by someone from the garrison during his preliminary meetings with the native. Stalker and Bone had volunteered. Time out of the sun.

'No, sir,' Lanné said. He glanced at Stalker and saw him smile. There was still some credit in that smile. It was still a roll of the dice.

'What's hypothetical?' Bone said, almost eager in his ignorance.

'Shut up,' Stalker told him, his gaze still fixed on Lanné.

Lanné could think of a great many things worse than the ability to accept change, but he did not want to confront his examiner so directly until he understood him better. Once, for instance, on the Mainland, he had seen a man trying to swim across a deep pool with a crocodile hanging on to his leg. He had seen another man and his wife take their own lives by chewing poisonous leaves and had sat with them for the whole day it had taken them to die. But this was not what the scientist wanted to hear.

He felt uncomfortable with James Fairfax's hands on his shoulders, the two of them locked in this gesture of cold avuncular affection.

'Because that is what everything is about, Mr Lanné. Change.' The man released his grip and returned to his seat. 'You do see that, don't you? You do understand your role, your own position in this very particular, one might say unique, scheme of things.'

Lanné felt as though he were being congratulated on some great achievement, the benefits of which were beyond his reach.

He had been surprised by the youthful appearance of the man, by the fact that he was so well groomed and cleanly dressed after his voyage. He had decided even before his arrival that he would think of James Fairfax only as 'the scientist', and in this way maintain some distance between them. That distance was now made greater by Stalker and Bone.

James Fairfax drew a ribbon-bound bundle of papers from his satchel and unfastened them.

'You see how well kept are our records.' He waved a batch at Lanné, and then in the direction of the two others. 'Every colony, every name, date of birth, family structures, whereabouts, known habits. Details. Details, Mr Lanné. The precise and comprehensive amassing of details.'

'And them that's still out in the bush?' Bone said.

'Here? Negligible, surely?' He had been told there were none.

These were the men who made up Lanné's shadow and who

whispered to him while he slept. These were the men whose distant voices drew on Bonaparte, Washington and Albino Billy.

'Negligible enough to slit your throat and beat out your brains. Kill your wife and kids and butcher your stock,' Stalker said. He half rose, as though about to make his point more forcibly.

Lanné wondered what this uncharacteristic provocation was intended to reveal. Perhaps he too resented the newcomer's intrusion.

'I am not here to concern myself with these others,' James Fairfax said firmly. 'Lanné here is the sole focus of my inquiry. These others are mongrels, surely, half- and quarter-breeds, little more than –' He stopped abruptly, conscious of Lanné, who raised his hands from his side and slapped them on to his knees at the precise moment of the unspoken word. 'I mean no offence to them, of course. But I don't doubt that a –' he paused in emphasis '– that a geneticist –' he said it slowly, drawing out each syllable until it was invested with a portent and a mystique of its own '– that a geneticist such as myself would find a purer line of descent in their blessed dogs.' He smiled to himself at this resolution. 'And what's more, I'm sure Mr Lanné here will agree with me.'

There were times when Lanné woke in the dark cold of the night and knew that these others were life and death to him. 'Dogs,' he said eventually.

'See,' James Fairfax said to Stalker and Bone, neither of whom was convinced.

'If you say so,' Stalker said.

Bone winked at Lanné and started to bark.

James Fairfax was keen to move on, and seeing this, Lanné said, 'Explain this to me.' He picked up the sheaf of papers which had come to rest closest to him and read aloud the title page.

The ease with which he did this surprised James Fairfax, who felt as though a telling, but otherwise harmless trick had been played on him.

When Lanné had finished reading Stalker slowly applauded him.

'Simply a gazetteer and directory,' James Fairfax said defensively. 'A listing kept and updated each year by the Protection Committee on the existence and whereabouts of all the natives. As you can see, it is comprehensive. Invaluable. My own work in particular ...'

Lanné examined the pages. The first few were filled from top to bottom with four columns of names. And then the columns were reduced. Each represented a different camp, each shrinking list an unspoken litany, until towards the end of the sheaf individual names floated alone in white space. Flicking through the pages gave Lanné the impression of a passing flock of birds, noticed only when their numbers were great enough to blot out the sky, and leaving behind them their stragglers, weak and lost and losing ground as the main body passed on and drew clear. He was convinced then, in gently closing the papers and laying them back on the desk, that he was right to keep his distance from this man. This man was the hunter with his rifle sighted on those stragglers. His own name was in there somewhere, perhaps forgotten in the twenty-six years since it had first been written, but there all the same, reducing him to his own targeted essentials and then leaving him unfinished in the expectant dash drawn between one date and that other yet to be added.

He saw from the scientist's face that he too was considering the same point.

For his part, James Fairfax felt frustrated, angry that this first encounter had not gone as he had expected. He had hoped to befriend this man, to get to know him in other than his physical dimensions and to leaven his report with something of his remembered history and humanity.

'My dealings with your brethren on the Mainland leave me in little doubt that there remains a great deal to be achieved here,' he said, retreating to the safe ground of accustomed familiarity.

'All my family are here,' Lanné said, caught unawares by the remark. 'Most of them dead.'

'So you say, so you say.'

'Dead's dead,' Lanné said.

'It is that,' Bone added, again warming to the proceedings.

'Perhaps I can convince you otherwise,' James Fairfax said. 'Who knows?'

But on this Lanné refused to be drawn. The man would be there for several months. There were still boundaries to be established. He, Lanné, was the emptiness in which this other had only just begun to wander and explore.

'I understand from the Governor that you live with three women,' Fairfax said. He recited their names.

Lanné nodded at each.

'Young women?' James Fairfax said.

Bone laughed. 'Three black old crows. Christ, they'll all be dead and buried before Billy here's half-way there.'

Again Stalker told him to shut up.

'So they're all beyond the age of ...' James Fairfax made a note alongside the three names.

'Only Eumarah's a pure-breed anyway,' Stalker said. It was not how men like Stalker normally addressed her and Lanné acknowledged this.

'And you choose to live with them rather than adopt the company of other men your own age?' James Fairfax asked. It was the first of a flight of questions. 'If there is anything I ask which offends you, then tell me immediately,' he said.

But that too would be an answer of sorts, the pen held ready for its tick or remark.

Some replies took longer to transcribe than others, and Lanné waited without speaking, the silence broken only by the whisper of the nib on the paper.

Walter George Augustus had already instructed Lanné on the most profitable subjects for discussion. Lanné remembered the visiting card he was supposed to exchange with the scientist.

'Finished.' James Fairfax went through the small ceremony of blotting the paper and screwing the cap on his pen. Then he turned his attention away from Lanné. 'Do you notice anything about my writing, Sergeant Stalker?'

'Such as?'

'I write left-handed.'

'Signifying what?' Stalker had written barely a hundred words in his life.

'Signifying nothing. It was merely an observation.'

'Cain slew Abel with his left hand,' Bone said suddenly.

'So he did,' said Fairfax, and he held up his hand and studied it as though some similar, hitherto unimagined potential had just been revealed to him.

Walter George Augustus and Mary Ann stood in the doorway of their home. Eumarah, Ruby and Pearl stood to one side of them, like servants.

Lanné had hoped that the couple would not be present, but everything he knew about them told him otherwise. He took a final drink from his bottle and slid it into his pocket. And then, remembering that it was not *his* pocket, he took the bottle back out, emptied it, let it fall to the ground, and in the same fluid gesture raised his hand and waved to them. Only Eumarah came forward to meet him.

'Been here an hour,' she said.

'They think he should have come back with me to see them,' Lanné said, motioning to the couple at the top of the white steps.

'Been drinking much?'

Pointless to lie to her. 'One bottle. Nothing spilled on the jacket or the shirt. Not even a ball of snot in his precious handkerchief.'

'Drink this.' She handed him a small bottle of aniseed cordial which made him suck in his breath afterwards. 'Say you and the scientist shared a toast.'

'To what?' Lanné said. 'To me?' To the edge of the abyss? To that single well-aimed shot?

They approached the house together. Ruby and Pearl waved timidly.

'They too thought he might have come back with you,' Eumarah told him.

Finally, unable to endure their exclusion any longer, Walter George Augustus and Mary Ann came towards them.

So complete was her devotion to her husband, that the previous day Mary Ann had visited Lanné alone and made the case for her husband going to the barracks in his place. She had even suggested that the scientist would have no idea of what Lanné was supposed to look like and that they would all be better served by Walter George Augustus presenting himself instead of Lanné. 'But this is history,' Lanné had told her with mock gravity. 'It can't be tampered with.' He had been drunk then, and this had angered her. Or if not drunk, then at least far enough down the slope on his backside for the rest of the inevitable journey not to cause him any real pain.

Walter George Augustus took back the suit, helping Lanné to undress and then passing the pieces to his wife for her to fold. He did nothing to silence Mary Ann's barrage of speculation and questions, ranged and fired in the wavering accuracy of her grievances. But nor did he participate in the attack other than to nod in silent agreement whenever her silences demanded it of him. He smelled the drink on Lanné's breath. 'Shut up,' he said eventually to Mary Ann.

51

'He's been too long in the sun,' Mary Ann said, holding up the shirt. She was quarter-breed and Mission schooled, but there was still a lot of Oyster Bay in her.

'Perhaps he might want to interview us all,' Walter George Augustus said, brightening at the prospect, and knowing immediately that it was a possibility.

'Perhaps if we offered,' his wife said. Her persistent, unquestioning agreement was beginning to disappoint him. Blind faith long since shrunk to blindness.

'Interview as in examine,' Lanné whispered to Walter George Augustus.

The moment Mary Ann made her suggestion, Ruby and Pearl turned their faces from her. Mary Ann took out a pocket mirror and studied herself in it, moving it towards and away from her face as though there were some perfect distance from which to admire her bloated beauty.

On the few occasions the rest of them had been invited into Mary Ann's home – usually to take Sunday tea, because that was what was done at Sunday tea-time, and because few of the others with whom Walter George Augustus tried to ingratiate himself ever accepted his invitations – Lanné had seen the three old women sit for hours with their eyes shielded for fear of catching themselves in one of Mary Ann's array of mirrors. Seen them sit with their bone china cups and saucers and silver-plated sugar spoons in their laps as though they were the detonators to their own small explosions.

Prompted, Lanné recounted all that had happened. Inquisition within inquisition until he refused to answer.

'Watch him,' Mary Ann said with a sneer. 'Him and his scientist will become big friends. Probably get invited to join a travelling circus together. Billy Lanné, Last of the Last. Get invited to the Governor's.'

Her anger, Lanné knew, was born of her own failure, and so he did not respond to it. No one else took her seriously, and

Walter George Augustus did not like to reprimand her too often in the company of these inferiors.

But she went on. 'Big important man,' she said. 'All the work Walter George Augustus does and *he's* the one gets all the attention. Big man. Everything he's done for you, for all of you, for all of us, all his Council work. Go on, deny it. You can't. He can't. Look at him.'

Everyone looked at her instead. No one spoke.

Sweat gathered in the creases of Walter George Augustus' eyes and nose and ran channelled round the moons of his cheeks.

Only to himself did Lanné admit that there was some justification for what she said. He also guessed that Walter George Augustus knew nothing of what had happened the previous day, and he saved this in readiness for her next assault.

Mary Ann's mother died in a fall from the Macquarie Gorge with the cries of the men chasing her in her ears as she went. It was said afterwards that Mary Ann's father, a ticket-of-leaver, was among them, and that he had more reason than many to see his wife dead.

It was not uncommon among the Bay people for the women to suckle dogs along with their children, and Mary Ann had arrived at the orphanage with a half-wolf on a rope.

The wolves were long gone from Oyster Bay, along with the devils and the tigers, but for many years, the years before the noose of the Black Line closed around the last of the people there, each time a wild litter was born everyone would wait anxiously and full of expectation to inspect the small soft bodies for the tawny stripes which seldom came, but which every now and then were revealed in some vestigial trace before these too faded for good. After this came the neck-wringing and the burning of the corpses.

Mary Ann's mother was descended from Cleopatra, mistress to the great man Robinson at the time of his Conciliatory Mission.

Upon first meeting Walter George Augustus, Mary Ann learned that he was in part named after Robinson, and this formed the basis of her attraction to him. For his part, Mary Ann was the first woman to express any interest in him. They were married six weeks after their first meeting, on the day she left the orphanage. She had been wet clay in Walter George Augustus' eager hands, and he had known nothing then of the useless and corrupting organ, of the terrible history she later intended to gouge out of herself and fling into some other, fiercer blaze.

4

L ANNÉ next met the scientist a week later. It was hard for him to say whose disappointment was the greater.

James Fairfax wore the same calico suit and hat he had worn previously, only now the suit was creased with wear. A flannel cloth hung from the hat to protect his neck from the sun. He commented on Lanné's clothes.

'What did you expect?' Lanné said. It was a cruel remark and James Fairfax did not pursue it.

'Are you a religious man, Mr Lanné?'

'Bible-taught by the Quakers, if that still counts as religion.'

'And were they good people?'

'All missionaries are good people. I thought that was the point.' Lanné checked himself from saying more.

'Quite.' James Fairfax sat back in his seat, turning to his papers before continuing.

It seemed to Lanné that even this slight rejection had defeated him.

'At Richmond,' Lanné volunteered. 'I was raised there, and at Schoutan. They tried to carry on at the whaling station, but you can imagine the reception they got in that company.'

'And how long were you a whaler?'

'Seven years.'

James Fairfax read from one of his sheets. 'You were lucky to find work there so regularly.'

'I was good at what I did. And cheap.'

'And do you intend to resume the trade?'

'Trade? It's work.'

'Still, it is an achievement, of sorts.'

'Quite,' Lanné said beneath his breath.

There was a short silence in which James Fairfax prepared himself for what he was about to say next.

'I have to tell you, Mr Lanné, that you do not conform to type.'

Others had said the same. It struck Lanné that the scientist might now consider himself to have been deceived in coming here, perhaps betrayed by his own eagerness and sense of commitment. This was reinforced by the man's next remark.

'Of course, in addition to my exhaustive study of you, I am also expected to make a full survey and report of the public work being carried out on the island to the benefit of all its inhabitants, settlers and natives alike.' He paused. 'Part of my instructions in coming here. The Committee.'

Public works, none of which would ever be completed. Booth's railway extension. The Bay signals. A new harbour, new barracks, new camp. Floodwater control – a joke become a tragedy – and proper sewers for the town.

'It makes an impressive list. Do you know of the work?'

'Only the railway,' Lanné said. 'I worked on a team blasting out the basalt under Mount Wellington.' Bonaparte had worked alongside him, and Washington, both of them in the simple disguises of other names and dumb silence.

'Tell me more.'

'Nothing to tell. We blasted it and blasted it and could have gone on blasting it from now to eternity and we'd never be through.'

'And yet the railway is operational. Quite a success, I understand. Especially in so backward and ill-equipped a place as this.'

'Runs right up to the face of the basalt,' Lanné said. 'And there it stops.'

'I believe there is talk of surveying a new route around the obstacle.'

Like this one, you mean, thought Lanné. Like me. 'Talk. The coal lies on the other side. Any other route will take the track into the bush.'

'Then you do not share the enthusiasm or optimism of the surveyors' report?'

'I doubt if my opinions give them sleepless nights.'

'No. Of course.'

On the Mainland, James Fairfax had encountered no one like Lanné. His direct questioning was leading him nowhere.

For his part, Lanné was confused by the sidewaters into which the man was only too ready to drift. Like Booth's railway, they were following a very precise plan, but succeeding only in going nowhere at great expense.

They were in the same overheated room as before, but this time alone. Men paraded in the compound outside. Voices and marching feet came to them through the closed door. Both men felt certain that Stalker and Bone would be somewhere close by.

'I believe our two friends have been asked to look out for me by the Governor,' James Fairfax said, smiling. 'You being an unpredictable savage, that is.'

'We could always meet in the camp,' Lanné suggested.

'Is this not convenient for you?'

It meant a walk of almost an hour, but Lanné was happy to keep his encounters with the man apart from the others.

'Risdon Cove,' James Fairfax said unexpectedly. He waited for Lanné's response like a doctor who has just prodded a pain.

'What of it?' Lanné felt unbalanced by the name.

'My apologies,' James Fairfax said, his purpose served. 'I did not mean to be insensitive.'

'Of course not.'

'It is just that the more accurate of our records, of our censuses, go back no further than the date of these ... of these unfortunate occurrences.'

'Is that what they were?'

'But you weren't even born at the time of –'

'These unfortunate occurrences. No.'

'I see. But other members of your family were involved? Perhaps the families of the women with whom you live?' He took out blank sheets and unscrewed the cap of his pen in readiness.

But Lanné was not yet prepared for him. 'Involved? Without warning, a man pulls out his pistol and shoots you in the head and you are said to have been "involved" in the proceedings?'

'Then tell me. It is why I am here. Did you think all I would want to discover was the length of your arm, the width of your nose, the circumference of your skull? Tell me. At least I can see that I have struck some emotive chord within you. Tell me, Mr Lanné. William.'

It was this, hearing his name, that stopped Lanné. He turned and looked through the window.

'What?' James Fairfax said. 'What? Am I not to call you William? I had hoped that we might become, if not friends – because I see the difficulties inherent in that – then at least acquaintances with a better understanding of each other.'

'To what end?' Lanné said calmly.

'To what end? To improve matters, of course.'

'What matters? There is nothing to improve. Nothing remains. That's the whole point of you being here, remember?'

'Then if not for you, for others. Whatever happens, whatever you believe, I assure you, you will not be forgotten. You are William Lanné.'

'And what exactly is it that people will remember me for? Tell me that.'

'We have all learned lessons from Risdon, from Burke's Hut,' the scientist said eventually.

'Learned what?' But the argument was becoming pointless, something as insubstantial and yet as chilling as the shadow of a cloud on a warm day.

'We must all eventually reach back if we are ever to fully understand the present.'

Lanné remained silent.

'Perhaps I might illustrate the point,' James Fairfax said. 'My own father, God rest his soul, was blinded. But before that he was a keen sportsman, a cricketer. It was his habit, so I am told, to kneel at the crease and say a prayer before receiving his first delivery. On some occasions, so confident was he, so contemptuous of the bowler, that he would take out his gold hunter, buff it on his sleeve and then hang it from his middle stump.'

Caught off guard by this sudden change in direction, Lanné felt obliged to contribute some memory of his own. But he had barely known his own father and so he told instead the story of Washington's father, whose first encounter with a white man had taken place in the valley of falling fires where the town of Marlborough now stood. He had been out hunting and was returning to his family in their shelter when a man on a horse had ridden out of a thicket towards him. Washington's father had frozen at the sight. The man and beast approached him. The man called out in a friendly fashion, but the animal snorted in fear. Unable to control the horse, the white man dismounted, tied it to a tree and continued forward on foot. He carried no weapons. Washington's father had heard of the whites, had known they were coming, but had not believed that they would be this white. Barely ten feet away from him this man held out his hand, and seeing the other's reluctance to reciprocate, slowly reached under his cuff and peeled off the skin from his wrist to his fingertips revealing the lighter surface beneath. Washington's father screamed at the sight of this sloughing and then ran without stopping back to his family to tell them what he had witnessed.

Only when he had finished the story did Lanné regret telling it. He felt numbed by it, as though it had not been his to tell, and as though some small but vital forfeit of his own past might now be demanded of him.

He was woken in the night by Bonaparte, who stood outside and called his name through the open window. There was no moon and the white circles on Bonaparte's cheeks stood out in the darkness.

'Sssst, Lanné, sssst.'

Lanné looked at the three sleeping figures around him. He saw the marks and then the dimmer glow of Bonaparte's eyes and teeth. Bonaparte continued calling to him.

He went outside, and as he emerged Bonaparte walked away from him into the darkness which ringed the house.

'What do you want?' Lanné called after him. The cold of the ground rose up through his bare soles.

Bonaparte carried on walking. Lanné ran to catch up with him, grabbed his shoulders and spun him round, angry at this casual evasiveness, as though he and not Bonaparte had done the waking.

'Been away a few days,' Bonaparte said.

'A week. We thought you were on your way back north.'

'Nah. Went into Kent. Been to Port Davey.'

A noise in the darkness alerted Lanné to the presence of others, and before he could speak, Washington and Albino Billy stepped forward. They too were daubed with white and came out of the pitch night like human constellations. The albino carried a saddle on his shoulder.

'You're in some sort of trouble,' Lanné said to Bonaparte.

'Not necessarily,' Bonaparte said. He avoided Lanné's eyes. 'Just wanted to know if anything was happening in town. If it was all right for us to stay here a few days.'

'Why shouldn't it be?' And then Lanné remembered the tale of the missing stockman. Missing on his way to Mount Picton,

60

the remains of his horse discovered, butchered, half eaten, half buried, the saddle missing. And as if to confirm all that he was thinking, the albino dropped his load to the ground and sat on it. His skin was grey in the darkness, and seemed to possess a faint luminescence of its own.

'Was it you?' Lanné asked Bonaparte, his voice a whisper, as though this somehow tempered the accusation.

'Found the saddle in Adamson Creek,' Bonaparte said. There was neither fear nor bravado in his voice and Lanné believed him. Only the grinning albino and the silence of Washington left him in some doubt.

'They think a stockman was killed.'

'That's what we heard.'

'Is that his saddle?'

'Don't know. Told you, we found it. Where was he killed?'

'Missing. Somewhere between South Port and Bathurst.'

'Then it's his saddle.'

'Better get rid of it,' Lanné said.

'Worth a bit of money, that saddle. Good leather.' There was no real conviction in Bonaparte's voice and Lanné detected this.

'Were you with him when he found it?' He guessed by the way he clung to his prize that Albino Billy had been the one to find the saddle.

'He had it when I met back up with them. Split up for a few days.'

'And you believe him?'

Bonaparte said nothing. Despite his otherwise wholly independent existence, there were still times when it seemed to Lanné that he remained a child, needing confirmation and direction, needing to have some unformed opinion or plan made solid before it was acted upon. This was most apparent when he was drunk and behaving childishly anyway, but the trait was most revealing and alarming when he was perfectly sober and yet still incapable of making even the most basic decision for himself. Like now.

'How was he killed?' Bonaparte asked.

'Want to make some guesses? Since finding the horse they've had search parties out as far as the Picton.'

'I think we passed one of them.'

'And it never occurred to you to hand over the saddle and tell them where you'd found it?'

'Bang bang bang, justice served.'

Lanné admitted the truth in this.

The sudden flaring of light in the direction of Eumarah's caused them to fall silent and then to watch as the flare dulled to the glow of a lantern.

'Where else were we going to go?' Bonaparte said. 'A few days here and we're headed for Launceston.'

'To the forest?'

'Perhaps.'

Lanné looked to the two others, who were now sitting side by side, sharing a bottle and whispering.

'They want to sell it,' Bonaparte said, his tone making it clear to Lanné that he knew this was not the thing to do.

Lanné considered the alternatives. Although the news had reached the town, the likely killing had taken place far enough away not to have excited the local men to their usual blood lust. The drought, the withering of livelihoods and the threat of fire kept attention diverted elsewhere. It was only a secure and confident homesteader who felt able to leave his family and his living and commit himself to a hunt. And anyway there were new regulations which somewhere in their rutted plains of small print now forbade bush courts.

It occurred to Lanné, looking at Washington and Albino Billy, that for them, at that distance, and in the darkness of the night, the problem had already been solved.

'I'm going back in,' he said eventually.

'Put you in a difficult position, does it?' Bonaparte said. 'You and your new friends.' He spoke more loudly now so that the others might hear him.

Lanné felt betrayed and refused to answer.

He left them, guided back to the house by the light of the lantern. Behind him the whispering men turned to grasses in the night breeze.

Eumarah was waiting for him.

'Bonaparte,' he told her.

'I know. I saw him in my dream. I was going to chase him away but you came to talk to him and there was nothing I could do.'

He stopped himself from asking her if she had seen the saddle.

She waited, as though expecting the question, and then said, 'I saw a hanged man against the brightening sky.' Her hands clutched at the front of her nightdress.

'Bonaparte?'

'I don't know. Too far away. I think the sun was rising behind him, but it might have been a fire. Either way –'

'I know,' Lanné said, and he went back to his bed and lay awake for the rest of the night.

When he went back out at dawn there was no sign that any of them had been there. Only the slightest crater where a man might have pressed his thumb into the dust. He recognized this mark and stamped it flat.

'So tell me, how is your work progressing?' The Governor sat with a napkin tucked into his collar and tugged at the wattled skin of his neck.

'My work with the man Lanné?'

The Governor had forgotten the name. If he thought of any-one at all as being the focus of James Fairfax's attention, then he probably thought of Walter George Augustus. If there was anything to be done in the camp, any news to convey, any new regulation to be posted, then it was always done through him. Why should he remember the names of any of the others? In addition, he despised Walter George Augustus and regretted that no one else had come forward to take his place as intermediary. It had occurred to him earlier that this man Lanné, considering his recent elevation, might be that replacement, but now, at the end of a tedious evening with the scientist, and with one ear cocked to the ceiling for his upstairs wife, he no longer cared. There had been other company earlier and the evening had started well. But most had departed by nine to be in their own homes before the few streetlights were extinguished.

'Lanné,' said James Fairfax, pausing to swill his mouth with port, 'is something of a disappointment.'

Cupid had been there earlier with his stories of the theatre. And then the Land Agent had arrived with his plans for the defence against the coming flood. 'Flood of what?' the Governor had asked him.

Now that they were alone, James Fairfax saw that the old man had little interest in anything he said, but he spoke anyway, if only to give voice to his growing disillusionment.

'He is not what I expected.' It was the safest beginning.

'Then why not pick another? God knows there are enough of them scavenging around.'

'But that would defeat the object entirely.'

'And what object is that? Tell people what they want to hear, always better in the end. More appreciative audience.'

A sudden noise above them turned both their faces to the ceiling. It was the noise of something being dropped.

'She will be asleep,' the Governor said quickly. 'Something fallen from her bed. A hairbrush, perhaps.'

It surprised James Fairfax to learn that the woman's bedroom was directly above them. Soft footsteps had come and gone all evening.

'You know by now, of course, that her health has failed her.'

James Fairfax nodded. He had heard countless contradictory tales.

'It is my belief that I shall be recalled to England at the earliest opportunity.' The old man spoke absently, as though he too were unable to rise to the surface of his disillusion and breathe again. He was the captain of a vessel whose cargo had rotted in the hold, betraying his poor stewardship every time one of the hatches was raised and someone looked in.

'I shall of course search out others with whom to make a comparative study,' James Fairfax said.

'She has a girl, attractive thing, to sit with her through the night in case she wakes in need of something. A sense of duty prevents her from sending for me.'

James Fairfax wished he had left with the others. He looked around the room. It had been his hope upon arrival in the town to find lodgings there, but no offer had been made, and when he had approached Cupid with the suggestion, the clerk had immediately told him to look elsewhere.

And so he had gone to Macdonald, a shipping agent known to Mr Mackenzie of the Protection Committee, who lived a short distance away along a path skirting the river. Macdonald lived alone. Two of his three daughters were being educated in Edinburgh, and the third supervised the running of a mission in Cape Town. His wife had left him when the youngest of the children reached fifteen, having gone from their home during one of his customary long absences. He did not know which had destroyed the greater part of him – the departure itself or the calculated delay of her preparations before finally going, first to Sydney, then to Auckland, then to San Francisco. Most of those who knew him now imagined him to be a widower and he did nothing to disabuse them. He never heard from her, never spoke of her. And just as he had endured the pain of this part of his discarded life, so he accepted now that none of his three daughters would return to him.

James Fairfax occupied two rooms to the rear of the house, with a separate door, a veranda and a small enclosed patch of garden. Macdonald's housekeeper changed his sheets and cooked his meals. Tea trees closed his horizon. Ferns, sassafras, myrtle and mimosa upholstered the veranda and bloomed early in the heat.

'Do you trust him?' the Governor said unexpectedly, pulling himself forward until the buffer of his stomach pressed against the table.

'Trust who? Lanné?'

The Governor poured more port.

'In what sense trust him?'

'To tell you the truth, of course. Most of them are born liars. They make no moral distinction.'

'I think so.'

'Think what? Think that you trust him or that they're born liars?'

'That I trust him.'

'Then you're a fool.'

James Fairfax was shocked by this abrupt change. 'From my experience on the Mainland –'

'That place! What are we to them – a backyard, a midden.' As suddenly as the Governor's anger had risen so it ebbed away.

James Fairfax did not pursue the matter. 'I believe Lanné when he gives a direct answer to a direct question.'

'Such as?'

'His history, his life, where he has worked and lived.'

'And what about his tales of this place, the people he lives with now?'

'He speaks very little of them.'

'Exactly. Keeping them away from you. Keeping you at arm's length despite everything you are trying to do for him.'

'I don't think so.'

'Believe me. They hide everything. Every trust is betrayed, every confidence, every kindness mocked and abused. Tell me, is he a drinker, this Lanné?'

'He –'

'Of course he is, they all are. Even that bore Walter Augustus. Walter Augustus – who in God's name gave him –' He stopped suddenly, aware of having said too much, imagining his words repeated to others, seeing his opinions in print, hearing the whispers preceding him home ahead of the ship which might never be despatched to fetch him.

'You will, of course, see my report, everything I achieve here,' James Fairfax said.

'Achieve? Achieve what?' He laughed. 'And I suppose like all the others you too believe my poor wife to be a madwoman.'

'I believe no such thing,' James Fairfax said, unprepared for the remark. 'Ill, perhaps. But mad ...'

'No need to spare my feelings. We here are all in thrall to the blessed Committee and its noble aims.'

James Fairfax struggled to make the connection. 'I can assure you,' he said, uncertain of what he might add. It disturbed him, the madness of this invisible woman, this echo of his distant uncle, but he could not explain why it disturbed him. There were still nights when he woke with the sound of his father's shotgun blast ringing in his ears, and again the connection, this persistent tie, was inexplicable and disturbing to him.

'You can assure me of nothing, Mr Fairfax,' the Governor said. 'They'll no doubt give you a medal for all this. Perhaps even a pension.'

James Fairfax had heard one account of the Governor's wife from Macdonald's housekeeper. The woman, barely twenty-five upon her arrival, had come out without their two small children, who were to follow in a year's time once suitable staff had been found and preparations made for their education. In the meantime they would remain in Suffolk with the woman's sister, who had sworn to write every two weeks with news of her charges. Even allowing for the time taken by the mail boats, several letters awaited the parents upon their own delayed arrival.

It was part of the arrangement between the two young sisters that, because of the vagaries of the mail, the envelopes would be dated in Suffolk and opened and read in the correct order upon being received. That way the mother might share in the month by month news of her growing children. She missed them greatly, and grew secretly resentful that her husband did not share in her sense of loss, however temporary.

Three months after their arrival two vessels foundered in Bass Strait, and although the mails were saved along with their crews, it meant that all hope of regular correspondence was lost. When the letters were finally delivered, after an absence of five months, the Governor's wife received a trove of a dozen, and knowing that she was unlikely to receive any more for a similar length of time, she heightened her enjoyment of these by arranging them in order and opening only one every fortnight until they were consumed. And it was in this way that she discovered that both her small children had died during an outbreak of influenza eight months earlier, and that for all that time they had lain buried, unmissed and unmourned by her. It had been a blow from which she had never recovered. Her husband, if such a thing were ever to be admissible, had mourned only for the loss of his wife.

'Ignore me,' he said, interrupting James Fairfax, who sat deep in thought. 'The ramblings of an old man. You must bring Lanné to tea sometime. He'd like that. They all do. Nervous as sparrows, of course, but it gives them something to talk about to all the others afterwards.' The old man never once took his eyes off the ceiling as he spoke.

At his next meeting with the scientist, Lanné was surprised to find a third man present. It was a man whom he had seen in the town, at the few Council meetings he attended with Walter George Augustus. He was a short, fat man, but with a thin, hooked nose, the tip of which hung almost to his lips and gave his otherwise flabby face the appearance of a sundial.

The scientist was the first to look up from the case of equipment he and this newcomer were inspecting.

'William,' he said immediately, holding out his hand and thus alerting Lanné to the small shift which had taken place in the company of this other. 'Let me introduce you to Mr Wooley. Although you are no doubt already acquainted.'

'A great pleasure,' Wooley said, but with a measure of reserve bordering on suspicion.

'Mr Wooley. From town,' James Fairfax prompted. 'Mr Wooley the photographer.'

'Among other things,' Wooley said.

'I invited him here so that he might make a photographic record of you.' He spoke as though he had just announced an unexpected treat to a child.

'Hands and head,' Wooley said. He closed the lid of his case and clicked both its catches. 'Profile and frontal.'

'I made a point of suggesting it to Mr Wooley,' James Fairfax added. 'He endorses the idea wholeheartedly. He shares in our beliefs.'

It was clear to Lanné that he had no say in the matter. His own role in the proceedings was made ever more apparent to him each time he and the scientist met, and he decided the time had come to redress the balance.

'The Governor himself is keen to view the results,' Wooley said, conscious of the need to promote his own part in the proceedings.

'Please, sit down,' the scientist said, arranging the chairs so that the three men faced each other. He had not expected Lanné to be so reluctant. He had employed other photographers on the Mainland and his subjects there had shown little reluctance. 'Mr McKenzie was quite particular in the matter of my – of our –'

'Mr McKenzie?' Lanné said.

'Yes. Mr McKenzie. Chairman of the Protection Committee. My immediate superior. I told you about him. Surely you remember.' He glanced from Lanné to the photographer.

'Perhaps,' Lanné said.

'I wouldn't do him naked without his permission,' Wooley said.

'What?'

'Not allowed. Not any longer. Not naked without written permission, signature optional. Not dead under any circumstances. Head and hands, head and hands. Family groups. I can do family groups. Most of my work in this line is of family groups. The Mission is keen to keep its own records. Mostly dressed, mostly mixed groups.' He wiped his brow and studied his handkerchief.

'I assure you, Mr Wooley, your reputation precedes you,' James Fairfax said. 'You need make no sales pitch here.'

The photographer was offended by this blunt reply.

Waiting a few moments for the tension to grow, Lanné said, 'Make as many pictures as you like.'

'I told you he would share my enthusiasm,' James Fairfax said.

'Six plates,' Wooley said. 'As arranged.'

'Where?'

'Out in the light of day.'

That would mean an audience. Lanné rose and went to inspect the equipment. Outside, he had passed the horse and cart used by Wooley to transport it from the town.

The next hour was spent in finding the best location for the pictures. Bright sunlight was needed, but not so bright that it would cause any loss of definition.

70

Eventually they chose a piece of level ground to the rear of the barracks. The side of the building lay in the shadow of its tin roof, but the ground a few feet away was bathed in light.

Wooley set up his tripod and camera, and Lanné posed, sitting and standing, inching towards and away from the camera until the finer preparations were completed.

A further two hours passed before all six plates were exposed. A small crowd gathered. Children were let out from the Church school to watch. They too might aspire to be photographed. Wooley and the scientist continually called for silence, as though, in addition to the light, this was some other prerequisite for the success of the pictures.

Lanné posed with each side of his face turned to the camera, looking at it full on, and with his face turned only slightly one way and then the other. For these two concluding exposures he also held up his hands for inclusion, his left palm towards the lens, his right pressed to his chest.

When Wooley had finished, and when he emerged from beneath his black cloth and drew the final protected plate from the machine, the crowd came forward to surround Lanné. There were a few dissenting voices, but most wanted to hear from him how he had felt during each of the frozen half minutes during which his likeness had been transferred to the plates.

Wooley concentrated on gathering together his equipment and standing guard over it. Children touched the legs of his tripod and ran away laughing.

Looking beyond those gathered around him, Lanné saw Walter George Augustus and Mary Ann standing arm in arm beside the gatehouse. Unaccountably, he felt suddenly sorry for them. Their home contained photographs of themselves, possibly even some taken by Wooley in his studio, but they understood as little of the process as the children now tugging at the photographer's trousers. He considered raising his hand to them, inviting them to share in the occasion and introducing

71

them to the scientist and the photographer. But instead he pretended not to have seen them. He sat immobile, as though awaiting permission to rise.

A party of armed militia entered the compound, and Wooley called for their assistance in loading his cases on to the cart.

Lanné, still angry at how he had been used, told the scientist that he had developed a headache as a result of sitting so long in the sun, adding that he hoped the pain did not manifest itself on the finished portraits. He said that if he had been given some warning of the occasion, he would have come dressed in something more appropriate.

'I think, for my purposes, your clothes are perfectly suited,' James Fairfax said, refusing to accede to what he considered to be little more than petulance.

Then Wooley called out to them that he was leaving. He sat on the cart with a switch held above the heads of the children still gathered around him. He did not use it on them, because that was no longer allowed, but flicked it deftly back and forth so that its slender tip cracked above their heads.

'Mr Wooley has offered me a ride back into town,' the scientist said. The offer was not extended to Lanné.

On his way to the cart, James Fairfax turned and called back, 'Three days. Here. Midday.'

Lanné shook his head.

James Fairfax stopped mid stride. 'What? Is something wrong?'

'Four days,' Lanné said, aware that if he was asked to explain this small postponement then his excuses would be inadequate and his resistance revealed.

The scientist considered this. He looked to where Wooley was trotting his horse towards the gate.

Lanné rose from his throne and wondered what, if anything, he had achieved by the gesture.

He left the compound later in the afternoon, after an hour in the company of Stalker and Bone, who had returned from guarding a working party sent out to repair the cliff top signals. A new wild mob had been sighted several days previously, and their appearance had put a fright into the labourers. Nothing had been seen since, and the two soldiers resented their day out in the sun.

Midway between the compound and the camp, Lanné again saw Walter George Augustus and Mary Ann, still arm in arm, sitting by the roadside. As he watched, unseen from his vantage-point on a higher path amid the trees, Walter George Augustus put his arm round his wife's shoulders. It looked to Lanné as though she might be crying, but he could hear nothing through the intervening trunks. Then Walter George Augustus withdrew his arm, took out a book from his pocket, and both he and Mary Ann started to sing, falteringly at first, but then with growing conviction. It was one of their hymns, and the familiar tune drifted up to Lanné like a bad smell. All this puzzled him until he realized that he had never before seen the couple when they believed themselves to be alone. Perhaps this was how they spent all their empty days when there was no one with them to be impressed.

After the hymn, Walter George Augustus took out a piece of cloth, unfolded it, spread it on the ground, and both he and Mary Ann knelt to pray.

As Lanné watched, trying to overhear Walter George Augustus' words, a movement further along the road caught his eye, and he turned from the praying couple to watch four men, naked and black against the paleness of the path, emerge from the scrub and cross into the trees on the far side. Each of them carried a bundle of spears. A dozen thin dogs followed them, as silent as the men in their sudden crossing.

Looking back to Walter George Augustus and Mary Ann, Lanné saw that they still knelt with their hands clasped, having seen nothing.

73

He tried to see where the four men had gone, which path they followed towards the town, but could make out nothing through the canopy below. Careful not to disturb the dead wood at his feet, he rose and walked further up the hillside until he too was lost to sight.

Ruby. Whose mother was tracked by hounds and killed in the valley of the Florentine when Ruby was a small girl left hidden with her sisters, some grown, some still children who knew no better than to cry out in fear and give themselves away.

She was taken home by one of the hunters, and when he had no further use of her she was handed over to the missionaries.

Her elder, pregnant sister was hunted out of Cumberland into Lincoln and trapped somewhere south of the Eldon Hills. She climbed a tree, breaking off the branches as she went. The hunters raced past the tree and then returned and found her. The broken branches had given her away. The men fired up into the tree until she was hit and fell to the ground. Then they killed her where she lay and one of them cut her open and pulled out her unborn child. That had been at the time of the First Line.

For twenty years Ruby spoke to no one. She was gathered up as one of the town strays, and later Eumarah took charge of her. For a further ten years all anyone knew of her was her silence, her unusually long white hair and the praying hands branded into the small of her back.

5

J AMES FAIRFAX unrolled two long scrolls of paper.

'The time has come for measurement,' he said. His eagerness had returned.

'Measurement?'

'This, Mr William Charles Edward Albert Lanné' – he spread out one of the sheets and weighted it at each corner '– is you.'

Lanné studied the bare outline of the man, arms and legs extended. It wasn't him, and he felt a sudden rush of relief. The man had neither genitals nor a face. At the top of the sheet was the single word 'Front'.

'Come closer.'

Lanné ran his hand over the rippled surface. A multitude of letters and numbers dotted the shoreline of the figure – coves and landing places scribbled on to some unexplored hinterland.

The scientist grew even more enthusiastic. 'With this we capture you for ever.'

We.

Lanné said nothing, waited.

'For every measurement I make there is a corresponding index. See. Forearm, F1, F2, F3 and so on. Length, circumference, mid point, musculature, external markings, colouring. Forearm, hand, upper arm, shoulder, back. Figures over your entire surface. This sheet for all your facing measurements, the other for your back. A new skin, you might say. And once each index is accorded its appropriate figures it then becomes possible ...'

Lanné stopped listening. He had become an alien landscape, as alien as the mountains and lakes on the moon. Feigning interest, he looked more closely at the outline and tried to imagine himself fitted into it. It was of a man with slender arms and legs – arms and legs unlike his own. Each hand was fanned, each finger slender and marked in each of its joints. He looked at his own hand. There was no excess fat on the paper figure, none on the stomach or thighs, no sagging flesh to weight a pair of jowls or fill out another chin.

'Let me see the other one,' he said.

James Fairfax spread the second scroll alongside the first. Identical in every respect except for the two squared blocks of the man's buttocks, each again with its fringe of equations.

'You measure me naked?' Lanné said.

'I've done it a hundred times before. No need for any embarrassment. Whole tribes have been recorded in this way. Small ones, admittedly, but there is no better way, no way more scientific or comprehensive.'

What James Fairfax did not say was that the charts had been his own idea, that they were what had brought him to the attention of the Protection League in the first place, and what had helped him to rise so swiftly into its higher ranks. He had brought science to the League like a man in a cold land cradling fire in his palms.

'No room for error. With each index accorded its due figure you will become completely known.'

'Where do you begin?' Lanné said. He took off his hat and unfastened his necktie.

'Not the head,' the scientist said quickly. 'The head and facial features are measured separately. The head and – '

'*My* head.'

'Of course. Your head and facial features demand – *deserve* closer scrutiny.'

As Lanné undressed, the scientist took from his satchel a

number of measuring tapes, some cord, pieces of chalk and a leather case of interlocking calipers, the smallest little bigger than a man's fore- and index-finger, the largest opening to the length and angles of a whole arm.

Lanné stood naked before him. He wore nothing beneath his shirt and trousers. Without realizing it, he found himself adopting the stance of the outline.

The scientist moved around him, wiping beneath his arms and behind his knees with a cloth. Then he took a piece of chalk and started marking various parts along Lanné's arm, continuing on his legs and lower body. Occasionally he made a mistake and erased the mark with a wet thumb. When he had finished he stood back, and using his charts as a guide he checked that all the required points had been transcribed.

Then he began measuring, repeating each figure aloud before recording it on the chart, as though the sound of his own voice were the only confirmation he required.

Turning to the mark centred on Lanné's chest, he measured first to his shoulders, and then along each arm. Each joint of each finger he measured with a compass, making fine adjustments as he went.

'Tell me more about your family,' he said as he stretched the tape across Lanné's back. He ran his hand the full length of Lanné's spine, causing Lanné to shiver and grow tense. Then he rubbed out the mark at the base of the spine and drew another. He felt for where the column of bones ended and pushed his thumb into the curve of the lost tail.

'My mother is buried at Tent Hill,' Lanné said. It was important to get the names right. His mother was buried at Sleeping Chasm, but this no longer signified. He had already related most of what he could remember, and what he refused to tell the scientist he would disclose to no one, not even Eumarah.

'And the Black Line?' the scientist asked.

77

Lanné felt him hesitate, squeeze the muscle at the back of his thigh.

'Before my time,' Lanné said, surprised that again the man should have made such a fundamental mistake.

'Then tell me what you know of it – what you might have heard from others.'

Lanné repeated only the tales which were already common currency. He could sense the scientist's disappointment. His knee was pressed back to make his leg rigid. The tape followed the contour of his calf and the compass prised between his toes. His foot was lifted and his heel and sole brushed clean and inspected as though he were a horse about to be shod.

'What else?' the scientist asked when he had finished the story of Ruby.

'That's all there is,' Lanné said. He refused to tell him the story of Eumarah's allegiances and betrayals. He knew the scientist was in no position to insist. His foot was placed back on the ground. Then he positioned both his feet on a sheet of paper while their outline was traced. When this was done, James Fairfax pencilled in the cracks and blemishes which scored the surface of the skin.

When Lanné's back was completed and the empty man fully marked, the scientist turned to his front. The curves of his chest and stomach felt tight against the tape. The scientist's dull monotone made it difficult to gauge either satisfaction or disappointment. The fronts of his thighs were marked and measured, but not his genitals. He scratched himself. Lint and dust floated to his feet. He felt a cramp in his left leg, and swung his arm to relieve the growing stiffness in his shoulder. His hands were traced in outline.

The scientist rubbed his palm and the inside of his fingers with an ink-soaked cloth and made an impression. When both hands were done he gave Lanné another cloth to wipe himself clean. Once dry, Lanné saw how the ink had dried in the creases and lines, bringing them into greater prominence against the creamy background. He studied these, fascinated by them, features of a land over which he alone held domain.

'You can get dressed,' the scientist said. He spread his scrolls side by side and stepped back to admire them – space become substance and the abstract equations now the measure of a man.

Lanné was pulling up his trousers when there was a knock at the door and Stalker came in.

'I said no interruptions,' James Fairfax said.

'We need the room,' Stalker said, dragging a chair to the desk.

'So? Am I expected to vacate it just because you decide –'

But Stalker wasn't listening. He went back outside and returned a moment later with another man, whom he held by his collar. He pulled this man into the room and then pushed him roughly against the wall.

'Prisoner,' he said. 'We need to ask him a few questions.'

Blood ran from the man's mouth and he tried to stem it with his tied hands. He looked pleadingly at James Fairfax, but not at Lanné.

Lanné pulled on his shirt and picked up his jacket. Then Bone entered. 'You not finished yet, Billy Boy?'

Lanné said nothing.

James Fairfax, realizing that all argument was useless, rolled up his outlines and secured them. 'I shall complain to the Governor,' he said.

The injured man began suddenly to cry. He pleaded not to be left alone with Stalker and Bone.

Still without speaking to any of them, Lanné left the room. James Fairfax called after him. Five minutes earlier, Lanné realized, and Stalker would have walked in and found him naked with the scientist on his knees before him.

He went down the corridor and out into the compound. The scientist came after him, still calling for him to wait.

Beneath his clothes, Lanné could feel the tiny chalk marks,

each one a thorn pressed into his skin, and as he walked he began to rub at them through the cloth so that they would not again confront him upon undressing. He picked up a handful of dust and scoured his palms.

He spent the rest of the day walking in the bush, circling the compound and the camp until he was beyond all sight and hearing of the place. He took off Walter George Augustus' clothes and hid them in a crevice.

He lay down in the shade of a boulder and slept.

He woke later to the sound of gunfire, and from where he lay he watched two men and their dogs chase a small kangaroo across the open land. He brushed the hot sand from where it stuck to him. Both men fired wildly at the animal zig-zagging away from them. It was the job of the dogs to bring it down and kill it. Unexpectedly, the creature turned and bounded back towards the hunters. One of the hounds caught it by the tail and held on, half running, half dragged by its prey. Then the second dog got a hold on the kangaroo's front paw and the animal was brought down. Both dogs savaged its face and throat until the creature was dead. Then they began tearing at its flesh until the men arrived breathless and kicked them from it.

Lanné sank further back into the shadow of the boulder, certain that he could not be seen, but unsure of the wind, and anxious in case the dogs picked up his scent through the gore which coated their muzzles. He watched as the men butchered the meat and loaded it into a sack. The dogs followed them away, leaping and snapping at the stains which showed through the sacking. He watched until they were beyond where his clothes lay hidden.

Afterwards he went down to where the severed head lay on the ground. He scooped out a shallow hole and buried it.

He returned to the camp at dusk.

80

Eumarah was alone and he told her what had happened in the compound. Most of the chalk marks were gone, but here and there on his back she found some faint smear to caress away.

'He asked me about the Black Line.'

'You could have told him,' she said.

The remark surprised him, but he said nothing. As a young girl, before her abduction, Eumarah had lived with a tribe who believed themselves to be the only living people in the world. They had some idea that other islands existed elsewhere in the surrounding ocean, but were convinced that these were populated only by animals and ghosts.

Each quarter, Leave and Application Day, Walter George Augustus and Mary Ann submitted their application to adopt a child from the Hobart Orphanage. They had first applied seven years ago, upon Walter George Augustus finally accepting that his wife would bear him no children of their own. He himself was one of fourteen children. Mary Ann did not know – she had been taken away too young – but she felt certain that her own vanished family approached this number.

At first they had been successful, given the children of other lost families. They were little more than wild things, even as babies, but Walter George Augustus and Mary Ann had once possessed great patience.

Then, in keeping with his rise in status and changes in the regulations, Walter George Augustus had requested a white child. There were plenty of these, too. And plenty more which looked white in their cots and then darkened later, whose straight hair curled and whose lips thickened only as they grew.

His application was turned down. Then resubmitted. Turned down again and appealed against. The unsuccessful case was heard in the court and reported in both the *Mercury* and the

Launceston Examiner. White women spat at Mary Ann in the street. She tried to persuade her husband that they had made a mistake in attempting to take advantage of the new regulations so soon. He struck her. And though he never struck her again, she felt that single blow each time he raised his voice to her.

Why couldn't she understand that they had been betrayed? There were rules, and rules must be adhered to. Why else had the regulations been changed if not for the benefit of people like themselves?

'People like us?' Mary Ann had said, puzzled, flinching as he slapped his palms against the wall beside her and tried to explain.

And so they had been given native children to raise, and in her own temperamental and unfulfilled way, Mary Ann had tried to love them. But her husband ignored them and made her work difficult. They no longer shared a bed. Walter George Augustus grew as pompous and as stolid as his name. And Mary Ann grew fat. In three years she doubled in size. It was as though, having misunderstood her husband's remark about 'people like them', she believed she needed to change and this was the most obvious and easiest way to achieve that change. Wherever she walked indoors the floor creaked.

Outwardly, little else changed. They continued to attend the theatre and civic dinners; they added rooms to their new home; land was bought and their garden expanded. They still went regularly to Government House; and later, when the court case was forgotten, Walter George Augustus was invited to Richmond and Brighton to help compile the Commissioners' Reports.

Mary Ann loved her small adoptees and then lost them when, one after another, year after year, Walter George Augustus insisted that they were sent out to the more distant Mission schools, and from there into servitude.

Mary Ann's heart hardened and she grew able to bear her

losses more easily. She hired a kitchen maid and a gardener. She paid small boys to run errands for her and to attend to her in her home. She went out less frequently. There were many days when she did not see her husband from dawn until dusk. She was still devoted to him, but increasingly her devotion was the devotion of lichen to its rock.

For his part, Walter George Augustus saw nothing to alarm him in any of this growing distance.

It was during one of his Testimony Hearings in Campbell Town that he heard for the first time the tales of Oyster Bay, of the suckled dogs and, later, the infanticides. He heard of the women who mutilated their faces with sharpened shells, of the babies born directly into hot ashes. And he heard too the boasts of old settlers who had lived with the tribe and fathered children there. Tales told over and over of how the women had been made infertile in the bearing of these half-breeds and then abandoned by their own men.

On one occasion he spoke to an eighty-year-old sealer from Three Thumbs who said he had seen Mary Ann a decade earlier and that he recognized her from this early Bay life. Walter George Augustus persuaded him to say more, revealing nothing of his own identity, and was then saddened to tears by the young and agile beauty the man went on to describe.

Nothing of what he was told did he repeat to Mary Ann, and he never once believed, in hearing these tales, that her loss was anything other than a tiny fraction of his own. She was the shattered crystal and he the man left clutching a useless handle.

'Caught the bucks killed the stockman and butchered his horse.' It was Stalker. He called to Lanné through the open doorway of the bar and then came out to him with a tankard in his hand. 'Six of 'em. Walked into Bathurst still with some of the rotten meat on 'em. Stupid bastards.'

Lanné did not turn to face him. Instead, he looked across the steaming flats of the Derwent, to where a line of carriages had drawn up. Music from a small band carried across the open space.

'They been tried yet?'

'What's the point? They had the horsemeat.'

'Might have come across it after the man was killed.'

'Why complicate matters? I thought you'd be pleased.'

The remark put Lanné even further on his guard. The word 'why' dried in his throat.

'Gets that bastard Bonaparte and his two killers off the hook. You can tell him next time you see him.'

'They're not killers.'

'If you say so.'

Lanné watched a group of young women walk barefoot across the mud and sand holding their bunched skirts around their waists, their heads swathed in voile against the dust. Several young men followed them. The women screamed and laughed.

'They're talking of an outbreak of cholera in Oatlands,' Stalker said. 'How long before you reckon it reaches here in this heat?'

On the far side of the river one of the young women tripped and fell and the chasing men caught up with her.

They stood around her in a circle. A short distance away, the other women, no longer pursued, stopped and turned back to watch.

'Sergeant!' It was Bone, calling from inside the bar.

'You tell 'em, Lanné,' Stalker said. 'Horsemeat or saddle, it wouldn't have made any difference.'

Across the river, the men were carrying the girl they had caught, holding her aloft, their hands the full length of her body as though she were a corpse they had just retrieved. They threatened to throw her into the water, but nowhere were the pools any longer deep enough to contain her.

84

Three days later word was sent to him that his next appointment with the scientist was cancelled. The man who brought the news could tell him nothing more. He was illiterate and handed over the folded sheet of paper as though it were a banknote. Lanné gave him the price of a drink.

Afterwards, because he had business in the town, he called at Macdonald's to find out the reason for the cancellation.

The housekeeper answered the door.

'What?' She peered through an inch-wide strip at him.

'I'm William Lanné.'

'So?'

He explained himself, saw the woman hesitate, saw her glance over her shoulder as though someone behind her was signalling a message to her that she was having trouble understanding.

'Mr Fairfax at home?' Lanné asked.

'Not to you, not to your sort.' She searched the street around him as though fearful of others ready to rush to his support.

'We had an appointment,' he said.

She laughed at him – whether at his use of the word or the possibility of it being true, he could not be certain. She looked slowly from his face down to his feet and then back to his face.

He wore only a pair of trousers which reached to his knees.

'Is he in?'

'No.' She slammed the door on him.

He knocked again, but received no reply. He imagined her standing with her back pressed to the door, one hand on the key, the other clutching the fabric of her blouse at her throat. He took several steps back into the street and looked up at the imposing house. A young gin, kinchin mott – a maid perhaps – looked quizzically down at him from one of the upper windows.

'Can you help me?' he called up to her, still conscious of the woman behind the door.

The girl continued to stare incomprehendingly down at him before fading back into the darkness of the room. He imagined he saw her turn, as though, like the housekeeper, she too was responding to the command of someone hidden. Angry at being denied like this, he cursed them both. And then he cursed the scientist.

Leaving the house, he made his way to the stock bar, and as he approached the entrance a man raced up to him from behind, collided with him and knocked them both to the ground. The man rose and ran into the bar. He had some important news to tell and started shouting to attract the attention of the drinkers.

Lanné waited outside. After a few minutes several others ran out, each of them shouting to the few people on the street. The first word Lanné was able to make out was 'murder'. He had heard it shouted out like that before, and each time he heard it he felt as though it had been shouted directly at him. It was the clap of thunder before a coming storm.

Waiting until the bar had all but emptied, the drinkers turned to eager messengers, he went inside.

The bartender stood by his barrels.

'Who?' Lanné asked him, leaning forward over the bar. And in that instant, vanishing as quickly as it had appeared, he saw the face of James Fairfax on his own shoulders looking back at him from the mirror behind the barman.

'Drink?' The man started pouring.

'Who's been murdered?'

The barman smiled. 'Calm down. You couldn't have done it. Up at Lomond. Ellenthorpe Ladies' School. Some girl. Violated, too, by all accounts. *And* they know who did it.'

Someone else in the bar called out to Lanné that he ought to go home.

'Why?' Lanné asked him.

'Because they reckon it's that mob come down to watch the work on the railway. People getting jumpy. Same mob went to see the mayor.'

'Mayor' was what they called Walter George Augustus. He remembered the men and the dogs he had seen cross the track by the camp.

'Not the same mob,' he said.

The man laughed at him. 'Don't see as it makes much difference, you ask me. They're going to send someone on his autumn stroll for it, tuck somebody up good and tight.' He yanked an invisible noose around his neck.

The distance to the school was over a hundred miles. He tried to remember when he had last seen Bonaparte, Washington or the albino.

'Violated something terrible,' the barman said, his eyes wide at the thought. 'Won't be long before somebody's rounded up for it. More than one involved, has to be.' He too put a hand round his throat and stuck out his tongue.

Lanné left the bar and walked out of town along the centre of the street. He could not believe that the news had come so soon after Stalker's revelation. He felt like a man who, having struggled to his feet after a fall, had then been maliciously pushed back down again.

Others came out of their homes to gather in small groups and discuss what they had heard. Someone threw a clod of earth which hit the ground and crumbled at his feet. He made a point of stepping in it as he continued walking.

He passed Macdonald's house. The front door was open and the housekeeper stood on the threshold. From the upstairs window the same empty face stared down at him.

He kept walking till he reached the open bush.

He left the track and passed into the spindly white trees which bordered it.

Mid-way between the town and the camp he climbed a tor

87

and sat looking down at the emptiness all around him. In the far distance he saw the pale screen of smoke where a bush fire burned. He shielded his eyes and searched for the flames, but saw nothing. He wanted the land to burn. He wanted it to burn in a circle around the town. And then he wanted the town itself to burn.

He was so engrossed in these thoughts that he cried out in surprise at the hand suddenly clamped on to his shoulder.

'Moving in the wrong direction,' Bonaparte said, indicating the smoke.

Lanné pulled himself free.

'Been burning a week.' He squatted on the block of soft red stone beside Lanné.

'There's been a murder.'

'Heard.'

'Where are Washington and the albino?'

'Gone.'

'They think in the town that you've gone with them. They think you're involved.'

'Can't have been: I'm here.'

This flippancy exasperated Lanné. 'They think you killed her.'

Bonaparte clicked his tongue. 'I know. I'm a nightmare. Can't shake off a nightmare. Night follows day and back I come.'

'Go back into town. Go *now*. Let them see that you're still here.'

'I could have run from there to here between then and now.'

'I'd back up your story.'

'You? Who are you? Anyway, you don't know where I've been, what I've done.'

Lanné waited for a moment. 'It wasn't you, was it?'

Bonaparte shook his head. He too had seen the wild mob, these four hungry men who stalked the same nightmares. 'All Dover-court down there. They'll find somebody. Don't need you or me to tell them what to do.'

'Are you leaving?'

'Running away? Don't know.'

'Go in the opposite direction.'

'I'd be guilty whichever way I went.'

'You should never have come,' Lanné said.

'You're beginning to sound like Lord Walter.'

Lanné signalled his apology.

The two men sat together in silence for an hour, occasionally looking up to watch the progress of the distant smoke.

When the sun began its descent towards the Derwent Caps, Lanné rose and made his way back down the slope towards the track.

He looked back before entering the trees and saw Bonaparte where he had left him. But now, sitting beside him, were several others, all of them gazing intently down at Lanné. The surprise of seeing them caused him to stumble on the loose slope, and when he regained his footing he looked back up and saw that the men – shadows in the clefts of the rock, a trick of the fading light – were no longer there. He started climbing back up, but Bonaparte flicked a stick at him to turn him and keep him walking away. And with that one simple gesture the distance between them became suddenly unbridgeable.

He continued down to the track, trying to convince himself of what he had seen, or imagined he had seen.

On the far side of the river a lone horseman galloped in the direction of the barracks, urgency after urgency, and in the still air the dust billowed out behind him like ink spilled in water.

6

I T WAS CLEAR to Lanné that James Fairfax had been ill. He
looked gaunt and had dark rings of sleeplessness around his
eyes. It was clear, too, though the man denied it, that he was still
in some pain. His jaw was stiff, and ached when he spoke, and
on his right cheek was a thumb-print of faded purple. Lanné
had not seen him for ten days, and this change in the scientist's
appearance surprised him. The man was exhausted after his
ride from the town.

'Time for your head,' James Fairfax said. He showed Lanné
the sheet upon which an oval was drawn, containing eyes, nose,
lips and ears. It was as empty as the outline map of his body
had been, and blemished over its entire surface with the same
minute lettering and equations. It was not Lanné, he could
see that, but it was where he would be contained, the source
of his re-creation – his resurrection almost – when the need
arose.

This time he was required to sit with his head in the embrace
of a craniometer, a contraption of rods and leather straps which
rested on his shoulders and kept his chin up and his eyes
forward.

He lied when the scientist asked him if it was uncomfortable,
and again when he asked if Lanné had any misgivings about
their work together so far. This last remark – the word 'together'
aside – put Lanné on his guard. There was something in the
man's tone, in his listless manner, which suggested that perhaps
he himself was beginning to question what he was doing. He

explained himself by referring to his recent illness. And this, he insisted, was caused largely by exhaustion and the heat.

He positioned a mirror directly ahead of Lanné so that he could see himself and watch as each angle and dimension was recorded.

This time the measurements were more comprehensive. Chin, cheeks, nose and forehead were all marked according to the equations on the chart, and each small piece of flesh, dividing joint and crease was plotted. Even the bedrock of bone was probed for and guessed at. The points of a small compass pressed into his skin until Lanné felt certain he would be pierced. His ears were held forward and then released and allowed to resume their normal position with the scientist counting off a minute before measuring them. Then he searched the stiff curls of Lanné's hair for his buried hair-line.

His final measurement, after an hour's exploration, a tape drawn around Lanné's head an inch above his eyes, seemed far too crude by comparison with what had preceded it.

'Reduced brain capacity,' James Fairfax said to himself, smiling and shaking his head at Lanné's concern. 'Except, of course, that you are an exceptionally intelligent man.'

Another disappointment for you, Lanné thought, and tried to nod his acceptance of the scientist's half apology. But movement in the brace was difficult, and he succeeded only in pushing one of the metal pins into his throat.

The scientist released him.

Lanné picked up the piece of paper and saw himself pocked with the scientist's scribble, his eyes and mouth in particular painted with unintelligible marks like those of a savage.

'At first sight it makes little sense,' James Fairfax said. The procedure, like that for the body, was his own invention. There was some point, therefore, in keeping the recovery of its coded secrets obscure. 'However, in the right hands it becomes the blueprint for your –' He said no more as he was racked by a violent bout of coughing. This lasted for a full minute, after which he sat gasping to regain his breath. Tears formed in his eyes. A small bead of blood appeared on his lower lip where his exertions had cracked the skin.

When the spasm had passed he wiped his face and dabbed at his mouth.

Flecks of sprayed phlegm appeared on the sheet Lanné still held. He felt it too on his hands and forearms.

'I promise you it is nothing contagious.' The scientist stifled a lesser cough with his handkerchief, surreptitiously glancing at this before returning it to his pocket. 'Mr Walpole has assured me that with rest and the proper diet I shall make a full recovery.'

Walpole was the doctor who attended to the Governor, and who supplied him with the palliatives demanded by his wife. Few others in the town trusted him. A month ago he had amputated the foot of a young girl who had afterwards died in screaming agony. He drank heavily and was seldom completely sober. He frequented only the bars where his credit remained good, where he paid for his drinks with advice and drugs, and where Lanné often encountered him. No one in the camp ever visited him, although he had long ago been appointed surgeon to the place and was paid an annual stipend for his duties there. He had become nothing more than another official presence, another shadow, another distantly reassuring signature on a form.

'Do you know the man?' the scientist asked.

Lanné nodded.

'Is he a good doctor?'

'We seldom have any need of him.'

'No, quite.'

James Fairfax needed to believe in his own recovery, and this belief would form a larger part of his return to health than any treatment undertaken by Walpole.

'The Governor speaks very highly of him.'

Lanné handed back the paper face.

And as though prompted by this, the scientist said, 'I have something to show you,' and took from his case a silver-framed photograph of a woman's head and shoulders.

'Your woman?' Lanné said.

James Fairfax laughed. 'You could say that. No, not woman – fiancée. We are to be married. The picture was made a month before my departure for Australia. Four years. I had hoped that she might join me there.' This small regret was overshadowed by the pleasure the man now received in looking at the face.

Watching him, seeing the smile form on his bloody lips, it seemed to Lanné that he regretted having shown him the picture, that he was now reluctant to hand it over, to share with him, however briefly, whatever it was that he held so precious.

James Fairfax dusted the frame with his cuff, savouring his fondness even further before passing the photograph to Lanné.

Her features were insipid and unsmiling. Even her lips looked bloodless, like the albino's. Her hair was styled in ringlets, fastened back over her smooth brow, but allowed to spiral forward in increasing lengths over her ears. It seemed to Lanné, considering the face for the first time, that it was unnaturally symmetrical, looking more like the empty oval in the scientist's folder than the face of a living woman. Perhaps this was her attraction for him.

'Elizabeth Mary Victoria,' James Fairfax said, apparently unaware of the irony.

'A very attractive young woman,' Lanné said, this being the least, and the most, that might be required of anyone. He knew just by looking at the unsmiling woman precisely what she would think of him.

'I had my own likeness made during the same sitting,' James Fairfax said. 'So that just as I might possess her, so she might also possess me.'

Strange words, but Lanné did not comment on them.

'Will she come to join you?' he asked.

'No. Her father considered it unsuitable. My own position before my involvement with the Protection League was uncertain.'

'And what about here?'

'Here? Come here, you mean? I wouldn't ask it of her.'

'Of course not,' Lanné said. He held on to the picture a few moments longer, ignoring the scientist, who waited only to take it back.

The woman's chin was ill-defined, fading without any clear line of separation into her neck. There was no life in her dull eyes.

'May I have it back,' James Fairfax said eventually, immediately reaching across the desk to take it.

It occurred to Lanné to tell him of the women he himself had lived with during his whaling days, of the one – a pure breed – he had intended marrying on Barren Island, the one whose beauty and accomplishments made another man, an old lover of hers, return from five years imprisonment to seek her out and kill her, and who in turn had been killed by the woman's brothers. Afterwards Lanné had sought for even the slightest measure of solace in all the wrong places. He had wandered for two years with the sole purpose of losing himself, and then for another two trying to find himself anew. He tried not to think of the woman, because even at that great distance her memory was still painful to him. It was another life for him, one he might now have been living. Only Eumarah knew the story.

An invitation arrived for Lanné, Eumarah and the others to attend a soirée at Walter George Augustus' in a week's time. The boy who brought the printed card stood in the doorway to the shack and called inside.

'Was just going to throw it in,' he said, indicating the envelope, which Pearl took from him. 'Only ...' He behaved like someone asked to throw a jewel into a cesspit.

Pearl left the envelope unopened, handing it to Lanné as though she too believed it to be the most precious thing in the dwelling.

Lanné had been expecting it. James Fairfax had been invited, along with the minor members of the various committees upon which Walter George Augustus sat. The scientist had been unwilling to accept, but was persuaded by Lanné, who told him that he was looked upon as the guest of honour and that Walter George Augustus would persevere. He finally agreed to attend only if Lanné and the three old women were also invited. Knowing the permutations of anger and embarrassment this would cause Walter George Augustus and his wife had made Lanné laugh, and it was only now, taking the invite from Pearl, that he regretted their ungracious inclusion in the affair.

Ruby grew excited at the news, but Eumarah understood immediately the negotiations which had taken place and said that none of them would attend. She said they all indulged Walter George Augustus and his fat wife too much, and that it was time to change.

'If we don't go, then the scientist may not go,' Lanné told her.

Eumarah considered this. Pearl became infected with Ruby's excitement, and so for their sake alone, Eumarah agreed that they would attend, knowing that most of the evening would be spent in the kitchen, or outside on the veranda with whoever had been hired for the evening to wear Mary Ann's wardrobe of maids' outfits and do the serving.

Lanné had the first of his violent dreams that same night. He woke with a cry and saw the three women gently patting the ground with their palms. The door had been opened so as not

96

to obstruct the flight of the dream spirit. He sat up and wiped his face, distracted by the reflection of the moon in his palm.

After watching him and patting for several minutes longer, all three women fell still and silent on the same beat.

'The dogs have it,' Eumarah said.

He could hear the howling in the distance.

Ruby went to the door and closed it.

'Once,' Pearl said, 'the spirits were lazy, and would seek out another sleeper rather than leave the room or shelter.'

His spirit, it seemed, had done the decent thing.

'Was it something to do with the scientist?' Eumarah asked him. 'The invitation?'

'Or Bonaparte and his heathens?' Ruby said, returning to them.

It was none of those things.

In his dream he had been sitting in the darkness beside a fire, eating a large piece of freshly-cooked meat. The ground around him was hard and stony and scattered with boulders and scrub. He did not know where he was or how long he had been there. There was a faint noise somewhere in the far distance, but the fire was too warm and the meat too succulent for him to pay it any attention. He sat and ate for what seemed like hours, until his stomach was full and it began to ache with the amount of meat it held. Perhaps he'd been walking all day, for having finished his meal he lay down by the fire and immediately fell asleep. Then, in his dream within a dream, he was surrounded by twenty scientists, all of them measuring some part of him, all making notes, and all of them growing increasingly excited at what they found. He submitted to their probing and prodding with good humour, and answered all their questions as accurately as he knew how. When there was no answer, he made one up. When there were several answers, he chose the most rewarding. They cut hair from his head and chest and drew blood from each of his fingers. They tapped his teeth with small metal hammers and held both his hands in trays of moist plaster to make casts. They bottled his saliva, his urine, his sweat and his tears.

He was woken from this dream within a dream by the distant noises which had suddenly grown much louder, and sitting upright beside the fire he was able to estimate how far away it now was, and from which direction it was coming towards him. He threw sand on the fire to douse it, but even as the fine grains scattered and sparked in the darkness he knew that he was too late. Men called out to one another, and all around them the baying and snarling of their hounds could be heard. He was in the path of the Black Line, no possibility that he would escape it, no possibility of the men not already having seen his fire. Strange creatures ran past him in the poor light, and a flock of small birds scattered overhead like blown leaves. His heart began to beat much faster and he rose from the ground ready to run. But the instant he was on his feet, he fell over. He tried to rise a second time, but a second time he fell back to the ground. He looked down at his near naked body to see what was causing the problem and saw with horror that one of his legs had been reduced to a bloody stump above the knee. At first he could not understand this. And then he saw the bones of his meal beside the fire, still with their tatters of cooked meat attached. He cried out in horror and shame and disgust, and for a moment the men and the hounds fell silent to let his screams clear the night. And then they started calling to each other again and the hounds resumed their howling. He wanted to pick up the bones and throw them as far as possible into the darkness, but he could do nothing except stare at them, swaying from side to side in an effort to keep his balance. It was then that he knew he could not escape. The Black Line had returned to seek him out and destroy him. The hounds were much closer now and he waited for the first of them to lunge out of the darkness at his throat. It was upon seeing the animal that he had cried out and woken.

98

'It was Bonaparte, his mob and the murdered girl,' Eumarah said, offering him an escape from explanation.

Ruby and Pearl accepted this and the three of them returned to their beds.

Before leaving him, Eumarah held his head and told him not to worry, that their dreams were not what they had once been. He refrained from telling her that his own had never been worth repeating even when they had been supposed to mean something.

He lay awake for the rest of the night. Nighthawks were calling in the distance, their choking cries, like the dawn calls of the Governor's peahens, too human for comfort. He knew that if he had gone to the window he would have seen Bonaparte, alone and watchful in the darkness. He felt as though the man was keeping guard over some small, unreliable part of him, as though he were the guardian at the far side of a hidden boundary to which Lanné was now approaching too close.

The Schoutan Mission Tame String Quartet played on the dead lawn. A block of yellow light reached out towards them from the house, stopping short of the low stage on which they performed. After repeated requests, Mary Ann agreed to lanterns being hung from the branches of the cherry trees beneath which the musicians stood. Their glow caught the dry leaves and the clusters of withered fruit.

'What do you intend playing?' Walter George Augustus had asked them upon their arrival four hours before the first of his guests. The lead violinist showed him the thick wad of music they had brought and Walter George Augustus picked out the few pieces with which he was familiar.

At seven, he and Mary Ann waited at the front door along with their hired maids, glasses of drink held in readiness.

The first guests arrived after eight: storekeepers, Land

Agents, Civil Officers, clerks from the Survey Office and the more recently appointed magistrates. The Bishop waited until only an hour before he was expected to send his apologies.

'Urgent business. Ecclesiastical,' Walter George Augustus read to his wife.

'Perhaps someone is ill,' she suggested, having missed the anger and disbelief in his voice.

'Or perhaps he got a better offer,' Walter George Augustus said. His first instinct was to screw up the headed notepaper and throw it to the ground, but instead he scored it along its centre, folded it and slid it into his pocket. He was wearing a new suit for the occasion, and an embroidered waistcoat tailored to fit the globe of his stomach. He longed for the day when he too would be in a position to refuse an invitation.

At nine, Lanné and the three women arrived and Mary Ann told them to go straight through to the lawn.

'Music,' she told Pearl, as though this would appeal to her and draw her through.

'What sort of music?' Lanné asked.

'European,' Mary Ann told him proudly.

'Does it matter what sort of music?' Walter George Augustus said.

'It matters to me,' Lanné said.

Eumarah jabbed him in the back. 'It was kind of you to invite us,' she said to Mary Ann.

Lanné was already half drunk, and as he passed them, both Walter George Augustus and Mary Ann sniffed deeply and grimaced.

'He's been drinking,' Mary Ann said aloud.

'Only because I've been to your soirées –' he invested the word with considerable contempt '– before and know what to expect,' he told her.

'If there's any trouble ...' Walter George Augustus warned him.

'Why should there be any trouble? We're all civilized, decent, hard-working people here. Look, we're even wearing shoes.'

Both Walter George Augustus and Mary Ann looked down.

Lanné raised his hand to a clerk he recognized. In the room beyond, a few people were dancing, and others stood around the walls watching them.

'Hard-working?' Mary Ann said.

Her husband regretted her inability to move in advance of any argument or provocation, to get ahead of it as he did and build his defence or a trap for it before it arrived.

Eumarah, Ruby and Pearl went through into the main body of the party. Mary Ann beckoned for a maid to serve them with cordials. She grimaced again as the three old women moved into the brighter light and she was better able to see the cheap dresses they wore. She traced a finger round the pearls which hung partly obscured by the lowest of her chins.

Walter George Augustus and Lanné stood alone.

'James Fairfax has yet to arrive,' Walter George Augustus said, checking his watch.

'So am I to consider myself the guest of honour in his absence?' Lanné said.

'You?'

'If it wasn't for me, he wouldn't be here. And if he wasn't here, you wouldn't be able to invite him along to this charade and pretend to be on terms with him in front of everybody else.' Lanné wondered how much of this he would have dared to suggest two months earlier, or if he were sober now.

'It's quite plain that you have no idea how to behave in these situations,' Walter George Augustus said.

'You're not the only one who's disappointed,' Lanné said unexpectedly.

'Oh?'

But before Lanné could add to the remark another couple arrived at the door. It was the dentist and his wife, a woman a foot taller than her husband and the mother of nine children, all living.

'William,' the dentist said, going straight to Lanné and not Walter George Augustus. 'Good to see you. Thought you might have died or something and they'd come for your bones. What is it they call you – King Billy?' He turned to his wife, who stood silently beside Walter George Augustus. 'Come and meet the abo king,' he said.

Lanné saw Walter George Augustus flinch at the word.

'That's me,' Lanné said, prolonging his discomfort. 'Uncrowned king of the abos. Perhaps they'll give me a house like this one and I can throw my own parties. Then you'll have to attend – by Royal Command. More drink, too.'

The dentist clasped his shoulders and laughed with him. His wife put out her hand and Lanné kissed it. She was genuinely flattered by the gesture.

'You'll not have to wash that,' her husband told her. 'Kissed by a king.' He nudged Walter George Augustus so that he too might share in the joke, and Walter George Augustus forced a smile. 'You brought that Napoleon with you, Billy?'

On a previous visit to the town, four of Bonaparte's decayed teeth had been pulled by the dentist, for which he had been paid with an uncut opal the size of an egg and the name of every winning horse at the Founder's Day races.

'This one's only for us civilized abos,' Lanné said.

'If you want to go through,' Walter George Augustus said. 'I'm sure my wife ...'

The dentist and his wife shared a glance.

'I'm sure she is,' he said, winking at Lanné.

Walter George Augustus was having difficulty understanding how swiftly and completely he had lost control of the situation. A maid approached with a silver tray, and before he could redirect her, Lanné took two glasses from it, drained one and held on to the other. He knew the girl and asked her how much Mary Ann was paying her for the evening.

Walter George Augustus stared hard at her and she remained silent. The dentist and his wife followed her back along the passage.

It was then that James Fairfax arrived. He walked with a malacca cane and wore a heavy coat. A butler was summoned to help him out of this.

'Mr Fairfax, James, you honour us, you really do.'

James Fairfax took a small package from the pocket of his coat. It was wrapped in marbled paper. 'For the hostess. Byron. An old copy, I'm afraid, but the bookseller here had nothing more recent. She does read Byron?'

From anyone else, the words would have sounded to Walter George Augustus like a cruel joke.

'Of course, of course.'

Lanné drained his second glass. 'She's very well read, Mary Ann,' he said.

'I thought as much,' James Fairfax said. 'The Governor speaks very highly of her, of you both. Is he here? Is he coming?'

'I'm afraid not,' Walter George Augustus said, hoping to suggest that the Governor was a personal acquaintance and that he regretted his absence as much as he, Walter George Augustus, did. 'A very busy man.' Anyone else would have avoided having to make the excuse by the simple mention of his wife.

'And you, Lanné,' James Fairfax said. 'It must be over a week.'

'You're still unwell,' Lanné said.

'But recovering,' Walter George Augustus said quickly.

'I would not have let you down,' James Fairfax said, turning to his host.

'Perhaps a seat,' Walter George Augustus suggested.

'Later.'

'Eumarah, Ruby and Pearl are waiting to see you,' Lanné said.

'Along with all the others,' Walter George Augustus said. 'Some quite influential people here tonight.' He wondered if he ought to offer James Fairfax his arm so that the two of them might make their entrance together.

'I look forward to speaking with them,' James Fairfax said to Lanné, adding, 'I hear fine music,' to flatter Walter George Augustus.

'European music,' Lanné said. He went ahead of the two men into the light and heat and noise of the party.

Some paused in their conversation at the entrance of the scientist. There were some among those present who considered his work there a wasted effort; others, not fully understanding the true nature of that work, and having read the *Courier*, repeated the opinion that if there was Government money to be spent then it would be better spent elsewhere.

And there were others who had heard of the cholera at Oatlands, and who looked closely at the invalid and then kept their distance from him. As yet, no cases had been reported in the hospital, although a farmer and his family in New Norfolk were already known to be suffering. Some wondered aloud why the man had been invited.

Pausing in the doorway, Walter George Augustus considered making a small announcement to mark their entry. But before he could speak, James Fairfax pulled free of his grip and crossed the room to where Eumarah, Ruby and Pearl stood together overlooking the lawn and the musicians. Lanné watched them closely as the scientist approached – noting too the man's slight limp – and saw the rapture on their faces turn to unease. All three still held the untouched drinks they had been given upon their arrival. As usual, Eumarah was the one to take a protective step forward.

James Fairfax bowed slightly and held out his hand to her. 'You must excuse my stick and my somewhat dishevelled appearance,' he told her.

It was over thirty years since anyone had last spoken to her with that voice. She held out her hand to him.

'Let me introduce you,' she said.

'Honoured.'

'This is Ruby, daughter of Teddeburic, granddaughter of Larrentong. And this is Pearl, child of —'

'Andromanche,' James Fairfax said.

'Who lived —'

'In the hills of the Little Swan.'

Pearl was at once flattered and alarmed by the man's knowledge of her. A change came over both her and Ruby at hearing these true names, and their timidity at the man's approach evaporated. They came forward, each of them looking around at the watching faces before extending their own hands to the scientist.

The maid approached with another tray and James Fairfax asked the three women if they wouldn't prefer something stronger than their cordials. All three said they would, and so he exchanged the drinks for them and the four of them touched glasses in a toast.

All this was watched by Walter George Augustus, and by Mary Ann, who had returned to stand by his side, where she belonged in situations such as this. She herself had not yet shaken hands with the scientist. She held her small gift but made no attempt to unwrap it.

'I told them to go and stand outside on the lawn,' she whispered to her husband. 'They said they liked the music.'

'Children,' Walter George Augustus said.

Eumarah looked directly across the crowded room at him and he knew she had heard him. He raised his glass to her and she did the same. Only when she turned back to James Fairfax and the others did he relax.

'See, against all expectation, he's enjoying himself,' Lanné said provocatively.

'He's ill,' Walter George Augustus said. 'Perhaps he ought not to have come. Perhaps he ought to be in bed.'

'Perhaps he'll collapse,' Mary Ann added.

'And perhaps he'll die,' Lanné said, as though finishing a rhyme and alarming them both even further. Only later, asleep on the ground as the night grew cold and the cooling earth ticked all around him and as rocks split in the distance, did he regret this remark.

'Take him a seat,' Walter George Augustus told Mary Ann, who left in search of someone else to carry out the order.

For the rest of the evening, James Fairfax, Eumarah, Ruby and Pearl remained the centre of attention. Others renewed their acquaintance with the three women.

Lanné stayed away from them, only too aware of the stories they were being seduced into repeating to the scientist. One glass of drink and he knew they would behave like the women who measured it by the bottle.

The soirée lasted until midnight, when James Fairfax rose, sought out Mary Ann and thanked her for an entertaining evening.

'But you've only –' she began.

'All you have to do is let us know when you are free to return,' Walter George Augustus said. He could hardly bring himself to look at the man.

Seeing James Fairfax struggling into his coat, Lanné offered to walk home with him. Eumarah and the others had already accepted the dentist's offer to drive them back to the camp in his carriage. He was working in the barracks the following day and intended spending the night there in order to make an early start. He asked Lanné too, but Lanné said he preferred to walk.

James Fairfax held Lanné's arm on their own short journey. He was exhausted, and on several occasions he stumbled, almost falling as Lanné braced himself to support the pair of them.

'You see, I have become the cross you bear,' he said, resting his hands on his knees. He coughed and saliva dribbled on to his chest.

'You shouldn't have come,' Lanné told him.

The scientist nodded. 'Will you return to see me?'

'Is there much left to be done?'

'With you, very little.'

'Then recover your strength and leave.'

'Perhaps in a fortnight on the Sydney packet.'

Lanné had not expected him to suggest so soon a date. But he also knew that the man would not be well enough to travel and that his departure would be delayed.

He left him at the gate to Macdonald's house and watched as James Fairfax climbed the steps and knocked to be let in.

For a week afterwards the scientist was confined to his bed. All his appointments in the camp and elsewhere were cancelled. Walpole told Macdonald that the white streaks which now appeared on the sick man's arms and chest were the unmistakable signs of scurvy, but that this was easily remedied. Neither man took consolation in the prognosis.

Lanné waited. The dying strains of the Tame Quartet could still be heard in the distance, distorted in the chill night air until the trailing notes sounded like little more than the discordant wailing of some nocturnal creature desperate to be answered in the darkness.

7

F IRE CROSSED the tracks of Booth's railway. The supports to a
bridge over a channel of the D'Entrecasteaux were
scorched, but the structure was left standing. A week later one
of these legs shifted and a line of wagons fell two hundred feet
to the ground below. Seventeen men were killed, all riding in
the empty carts, some still roped to them ready to start hauling
back. An engine sat uselessly in the town two miles from the
buffer end of the track.

Twelve of the bodies were retrieved the next day when the
crushed wagons were searched. Two other men were found
alive, but both died of their injuries on the ride back into town.
The three remaining corpses were lost to either the fire or the
water and were never recovered.

There was an argument in the Council concerning the repair
of the bridge, but eventually it was decided that the structure
would be rebuilt a short distance inland and the track lifted and
relaid to cross it.

Despite being confined to his room, James Fairfax took a great
interest in the accident and its aftermath, and he sent a message for
Lanné to visit him and tell him everything he could find out about
it. Nowhere in the newspaper reports did he read that any of the
dead men had still been harnessed to the wagons. No move was
ever made to extend the track in the direction of its waiting engine.

Lanné arrived late in the afternoon. He expected to be
greeted by the sour housekeeper, but Macdonald himself let
him in.

'How is he?'

Macdonald put a finger to his lips and shook his head.

James Fairfax called out to them from the rear of the house, and Macdonald indicated the dark corridor, its walls filled with pictures and framed photographs, leading to it.

Lanné was the first to enter.

The scientist was sitting up in bed. His hair was unbrushed and hung over his forehead. He smoothed it away from his eyes, leaving it plastered across his brow. He pushed himself up on his pillows. On the bed and surrounding chairs and floor were scattered books and papers, some of which Lanné recognized from his visits to the barracks.

'What of the railway?' James Fairfax asked immediately.

'I'll fetch you a drink,' Macdonald said. 'Leave you alone with Mr Lanné here.'

Lanné went to the bed and cleared one of the chairs of its debris.

There were fresh bruises on the scientist's cheeks, and these now extended to his throat and neck. One of his teeth had come out, leaving a gap at the front.

James Fairfax shivered and pulled shut his collar. His nightshirt was stained with sweat, and soiled cloths lay soaking in a bowl set on a cabinet beside the window.

'Perhaps I overexerted myself. No matter. Walpole assures me of my eventual recovery.'

'Perhaps,' Lanné told him. He turned his attention to the array of pots and bottles beside the bed, to the pestle and mortar still with its smear of paste, and to the half-filled syringe which lay beside it. And amid all this stood the silver-framed photograph of the unsmiling fiancée, her gaze condemning the room and everyone in it.

'Walter George Augustus,' James Fairfax said, drawing Lanné back to him. 'Do something to stop him and his wife from visiting me. They come every day. I've started feigning sleep to

110

avoid them.' He laughed at this, but the laughter quickly turned to a wheeze in his throat.

Holding him, Lanné felt the man's spine and the plates of his shoulder-blades through the thin material of his nightshirt.

'You aren't the first to regret accepting one of their invitations,' Lanné said dispassionately. 'I'll tell them to stop coming.'

It was more than James Fairfax wanted, but he could do little more than raise his hand in assent.

Macdonald returned with a tray of drinks and set it down on the bed between the two men. For James Fairfax there was a small bowl of beef tea, of which he drank little.

Lanné repeated all he had heard about the railway accident. And then about the hunt for the killers of the schoolgirl. It was by then common knowledge that Albino Billy and Washington were responsible, and, by implication, Bonaparte. Lanné had already made an appeal on his behalf to both the Governor and the Police Superintendent, but neither man, despite their assurances, had believed him. Blood still needed to be let.

Lanné left an hour later. James Fairfax had by then fallen into a troubled sleep, and Lanné spent the rest of his time there with Macdonald. He too understood the worthlessness of Walpole's treatment, and he was concerned now about his own position in the proceedings. A batch of a dozen letters had arrived from the Protection League in Sydney, and attached to these were four from England.

Lanné left and went to see Walter George Augustus. But he was not at home and so he told Mary Ann that the scientist was no longer well enough to receive visitors. She accused him of lying. She said he was jealous of her husband's ability to talk with the man as an equal. Lanné refused to be provoked.

He left her and she continued calling after him. People in the street stopped to look. There was a smell of burning in the air.

Eumarah found him at the stockyards where a sheep sale was under way, and where he stood at the front of the ring surrounded by herders and slaughtermen. By then whole flocks were being driven in to town starving to be reduced to cheap tallow. It was no real limit to loss. She pushed through to stand beside him. Most of those present knew her and made way for her. A man pulled a small clean fleece from a bundle he carried and gave it to her. Twenty years earlier she had nursed his children, and every time he saw her he repaid her in some way.

Lanné felt the tug at his sleeve. Normally he felt easy in the company of these men, but now their disappointments had turned some of them murderous. Most only came into town once a year, but gathered in disaster, their grazing turned to dust, their frustration and anger were being distilled and this made them unpredictable. He followed Eumarah to the back of the crowd.

'Pearl,' she said. 'She came home with some bad news. A death. She wanted me to find you. Ruby is with her. She's inconsolable.' She spoke in a whisper, her head bowed.

'What does she want me to do? Who is it?'

'Man called Rowlebauna Third.'

Lanné knew the man. 'Son of Achilles?'

She pulled him further from the herders and the stockmen. She too felt uneasy amid their restlessness. 'Him and Pearl were rounded up together on the Douglas. She lived with him. She was his wife.'

'But that must have been forty years ago.'

'It was.'

The man had been brought to town a year earlier. Lanné had known nothing of Pearl's distant involvement with him.

'He's been sick. No other family. Crippled in a chase. She's been going to sit with him, to talk, for the past six months.'

'She never mentioned him.'

'She told no one. She was ashamed. She thought he was dead until he showed up here. She had two of his children, both dead.'

It sometimes occurred to Lanné that he knew nothing at all about these old women.

'What does she want me to do?'

'He's been taken to the mortuary. He's a pure-breed. She's afraid they're going to send him away. She's confused.' All the time she spoke she was leading him out of the stockyards and into the street.

The mortuary stood only a short distance away. It was little more than an underground room which also served as a rear entrance to the hospital.

Upon arrival, Eumarah sent Lanné on alone. She stood twenty feet behind him as he knocked. There was no answer. He knocked again. Still no reply. He turned to her and shrugged, but she motioned for him to try again. This time the door opened as he raised his knuckles to it.

Lanné explained the purpose of their visit to the man who stood before him.

'Who sent you?'

'I'm family,' Lanné lied.

The man laughed. 'You don't know the meaning of the word. What are you – son or grandson? He's as old as Methuselah so you aren't his brother.'

'Son,' Lanné said firmly.

The man stopped laughing. He wore gauntlets and a dirty leather apron to his ankles.

Lanné pressed home his advantage. 'Come to take him home for burial.'

'Where's that, then?'

'Circular Head,' Eumarah called out.

'And who's she? His woman?'

'Sister,' Lanné said.

'Circular Head. Closed that cesspit down years ago. The place is rife. You can't bury him there. Anyhow, I need to see a letter of authorization before you can take him anywhere.'

'I still want to see him,' Lanné said.

The man hesitated before opening the door wider and stepping aside.

'I'm not the mortician,' he said when the three of them were inside and descending the stone stairs into the cool chamber below. 'Assistant. Senior assistant. As good as a mortician. It's me who'll be carrying out all the necessary on our friend here.'

'Rowlebauna,' Lanné said.

'What? Oh, I see. I knew it was something too fancy.' He led them through to the corpse.

The old man lay on his back, his crippled legs bent outwards.

'How you going to take him if and when you get permission?'

This had not occurred to Lanné. 'I've hired a cart to come and collect him. I'm only here to make sure nothing's happened to him.'

'He's dead. How can anything happen to him?'

But by the way he spoke, Lanné knew the man understood him.

'You think we still send their heads off to Sydney? You think anyone still cares enough?' He lit a second lantern and looked more closely at Lanné. 'Here, I know you. You're the one thinks he's something special. You're the one they're making all that fuss about.'

'Not me,' Lanné said.

'You look like him,' the man said sceptically.

'His name's William Lanné,' Lanné said.

'That's it – King Billy.'

'So how can it be me?' The ease of this denial pleased him. He walked around the naked bony corpse. It might have been the old man he had seen asleep on the side of the road when he and Eumarah had walked beside the abandoned quays.

'Want to see something?' the man said, keen to reassert himself. He took his lantern to a wall of cupboards and from one of these he took out a heavy glass jar. Lanné remained beside the body on the table and it was difficult for him to see what the jar contained. But he knew it was something to shock him and so he braced himself against the revelation, unwilling to concede even this small advantage to the man.

Eumarah ran her hands over the corpse and murmured. This, Lanné realized, was the true purpose of their visit. It would be a short, efficient prayer.

The man came back to him, his lantern balanced on the lid of the jar.

'What do you say to that?'

Eumarah collected last visions from the closed eyes.

In the jar was a head, black but pickled grey, shaved of its hair and beard, and frayed at the neck where it had been severed. An open mouth and staring eyes.

'He come from Glamorgan when they cleared the place out. Probably tried to leg it. Nice looking specimen, don't you think?'

The head rose and fell slightly in its sustaining liquid. It was the first Lanné had seen, but he was not repulsed by it, and he knew that, perversely, he had more in common with the man whose head it had once been than with the man who now held it.

Behind him Eumarah stopped murmuring and called to him.

'Bet you want to know why we keep it, eh?' The man had expected much more.

'Not particularly,' Lanné said.

'Yes you do. He's one of you. You must do.'

Indicating the corpse, Lanné said, 'Make sure he stays here until the cart arrives.'

He took Eumarah's hand and led her back up the steps and out into the sunlight.

Pausing in the doorway, he looked back, and it seemed to him now as though the man in the long apron were holding his own head in the jar, his eyes magnified wide with surprise, his mouth gaping with the words he could not think to shout.

Bonaparte returned three nights later and beckoned Lanné from his dreamless sleep.

Barely awake, Lanné rose and went to the window where Bonaparte stood. Behind him waited half a dozen others. He searched for Washington and the albino, but neither was there; this was the same mob Bonaparte had arrived with from Falmouth eight weeks earlier.

'What do you want?' Lanné whispered.

'Going on a visit to the Coal River settlement. Want to come?'

In their youth, Lanné and Bonaparte had visited Coal River every summer. It was where what remained of Bonaparte's family were taken after the Second Black Line. They had last made the visit together three years ago, after an absence of a decade, during which even those few living remnants had perished.

'There's nothing there,' Lanné said.

Behind him, Pearl turned in her bed and spoke in her sleep.

'Gone a week,' Bonaparte said.

Without fully understanding why, the idea of a week's unexplained absence appealed to Lanné.

Bonaparte took several paces back and the others moved forward to surround him.

'Are you going like that?' Lanné asked him, indicating Bonaparte's markings. It was widely believed by the English that only the wild men still painted themselves in this way. To wear the paint in town, in daylight, was unheard of.

Bonaparte held out a pot of paint in answer.

'I'll need to collect a few things.'

116

'No. Come now. Come before you're fully awake.'

A dream start, thought Lanné, remembering how they had gone in the past. The idea became even more appealing to him.

He climbed through the window and fell to the ground at Bonaparte's feet. The others walked off ahead of them.

Lanné painted himself. It was an hour before dawn and the sky in the direction of the unrisen sun was already brightening.

On the first day they crossed the Fingertips Plain.

The others went ahead and hunted and brought back part of their catch to Bonaparte. They dug up roots and found a nest of frogs, from which they all sucked water before eating the meat. For several minutes they stood amid a drift of low-flying parakeets, barely able to move without bringing the birds to the ground.

'What is there left?' Lanné asked as the storm passed away, increasingly aware of his uncertain need to explain the journey.

'Not much,' Bonaparte told him. He gazed ahead as he spoke, as though he were seeing all that he described. 'Most of the stonework they dismantled for ballast. Graveyard's still there. Still a signal station.'

Lanné tried to remember the camp as it had been on his last visit. Two hundred men, women and children had been brought to it, most from Swan Island, where they had sulked and died like koalas, and some, the children, from Puer Point, where that particular experiment had also failed.

Coal River had been constructed in advance. Smallpox came the first year, dysentery the second. A garrison of eighteen men died in four days. A dispensary was promised but never built. It was from the Coal River graveyard that Bonaparte and his mob had retrieved the last of their bodies.

On the second day they turned south and crossed empty grassland, coming at last to a cluster of abandoned silver workings, each site marked with its own small crop of crosses.

On the third day Lanné and Bonaparte parted from the oth-

117

ers, who turned towards Bathurst, and the two men walked into the Pitt Water salt pans, where Bonaparte searched for and retrieved a stash of drink. They settled in the shade of a copse of wattle trees and spent the rest of the day and night there. By Lanné's reckoning they were only five or six miles from Coal River. He asked Bonaparte why they didn't complete their journey and spend the night there, but Bonaparte became evasive.

The following morning Lanné woke stiff and hungover.

He was alone.

He called for Bonaparte, but received no reply. He could no longer sieve the birdsong for its one human note. He cursed the man, believing himself to have been abandoned with as much consideration as Bonaparte threw away his empty bottles.

An hour later, hungry and thirsty, he set off in the direction of Coal River. He dug where he thought he might collect water, but found none.

He walked for four hours and was surprised that he did not come in sight of the empty settlement. It occurred to him that he had walked in a circle, but then he dismissed this as ridiculous; the sun was still to his right. As youths he and Bonaparte had made the journey with only a single overnight stop.

Hot and disorientated, he sat down to wait.

It had been a week since he had last seen the scientist and he now felt himself drawing away from the man and his expectations. Reports of James Fairfax's health reached him via Walter George Augustus, but these were in turn tempered by *his* own disappointment. Overall there appeared to have been little change, stability perhaps, a slight improvement. The Sydney mail boat had come and gone and he had not gone with it.

While he waited – for what or who he did not know – he began to pick at the paint on his arms and legs. The dried flakes plucked the hairs from his shins. For the first time in many years, lost though he was, he felt in full control of his life, as though he alone might decide on the path ahead of him.

After a while, he slept.

He woke late in the afternoon and saw a distant figure approaching him through the haze, melting and reforming in the sulphur-coloured expanse, dissolved in the heat and then taking shape as it came closer. His first instinct was to hide, but he was at the centre of the plain and the nearest cover lay miles away. And so he crouched down and waited.

The figure continued towards him, and only when it approached within twenty yards of him did he recognize Bonaparte. He was painted differently, scarlet and ochre instead of white, and he was carrying a sack.

Lanné called out to him.

'What's wrong? Something happen?' Bonaparte said, surprised by Lanné's anger at being left behind.

'You abandoned me in the middle of nowhere.'

'Nowhere? You even sound like them. I went on alone, that's all. How much have you forgotten?'

'Where are the others?'

Again Bonaparte became evasive. He lowered the sack to the ground, and from the sound it made as it settled, Lanné knew it was full of bones.

'From the graveyard?'

Bonaparte nodded. 'One last time.'

'Where are you taking them?'

'Back where they belong.'

Neither man spoke for a moment. To be found in possession of the bones was punishable by imprisonment. When Bonaparte had first started retrieving them, the crime had carried the death penalty.

Lanné looked hard at the sack, imagining its contents, and wondering if he were brave enough to pick it up and throw it over his own shoulder.

He sensed that something else was being kept from him. He began to wonder why Bonaparte had been so insistent on

119

him joining them only to be abandoned so close to their goal.

'How was the place?' he asked him.

'Empty.'

And then Lanné realized. 'And how are Washington and the white man?'

Bonaparte made no attempt to deny that this was where the two hunted men were now in hiding.

A sense of urgency overcame Lanné and he looked back along the line of his own tracks, only too evident where they had broken through the crystalline crust.

Bonaparte picked up the sack of bones and started walking back in the direction they had come.

They passed the copse where they had spent the previous night, and walked until sunset, climbing into the foothills, until Bonaparte, who knew the district, led them into a narrow gorge, at the end of which was a low cave, its entrance concealed by a cone of loose scree.

The place had been recently used. The embers of several fires stained the floor, and men and animals paraded the walls. The desiccated corpse of a wallaby dangled from the ledge where it had been hung, and the skulls and scattered bones of other meals lay beneath it.

Bonaparte kindled a small fire and the smoke rose into a crack in the roof.

Later, after they had eaten, Lanné said, 'Did they kill her, the girl?'

Bonaparte nodded.

'Why?'

'Said she was lost and they found her.'

'But there might have been a reward.' There was, and the albino had taken it.

'Said they took her back to the road, no trouble, but once she knew where she was she started calling them names. Said she spat on them.'

'How did she come to be lost?'

'Washington said he thought she'd run off from the school and then got scared and changed her mind. It wasn't him who did any of those things to her.'

'The albino.'

Bonaparte nodded.

'They'll hang for it.'

Bonaparte nodded again and the painful confession was over.

Lanné wished now that he'd been brave enough to pick up and carry the bones, to share even that small part of the other man's burden.

At first he could not tell where he lay – whether in his bed, on the ground outside, or on a surface even colder and less giving. He believed he had cried out – as he had cried out at the leaping hound – and that this was what had woken him. He felt a hand on his arm and heard whispering voices in the darkness around him. But when he tried to push himself up to discover who was there, he found himself unable to rise. He called out to ask what was happening, but no one answered him. He felt a wetness on his cheeks and wondered if he had been crying in his sleep, or if he was crying now, and what the cause of his pain or sorrow might be. He could recollect no nightmare, had brought no persistent fragment of this with him into the uncertain state between sleep and full waking in which he was now suspended.

He heard the whispering voices again, and this time they fell silent at his shout, reassuring him that he had at least been heard. They were the voices of men, refined voices, formal, English voices, but voices he had never before heard.

This time he tried to rise by first bending his legs, but these too were restrained. He was held down at the ankles and wrists, and though he could not see them, he could feel even broader straps across his chest and waist. He was naked and could not even raise a hand to cover himself.

A face appeared in the darkness directly above him. Further back a lantern was lit and the face looked down at him wreathed in the dull yellow glow. He expected to recognize the scientist, but this man was older, with white hair and a full beard. He wore a collarless shirt and a pair of vivid white gloves. He spread and flexed his fingers as though he were about to play the piano.

You do not know me, Mr Lanné, this man said to him.

Lanné could not answer. His lips were dry, his tongue leaden in his mouth.

You cannot speak, the man said. Anaesthetic. Crude, but ...

Another man appeared beside him, younger, with a long sallow face. He too wore gloves. He held something out to the older man, and only when the lantern was brought closer did Lanné see that it was a scalpel.

Our turn now, Mr Lanné.

A smile. One way or another we must succeed with you. Our options, as I know you understand, are greatly reduced. He wrote the words in the air with the scalpel as though it were a pen.

Truly, you will feel nothing, Mr Lanné, the white-haired man said.

Or almost nothing.

Strangely, the only thought in Lanné's head was to demand to know who had told them his name.

A third and a fourth and a fifth face appeared, all of them eager to look down at him. Someone inspected his feet, his arms and his legs. Another ran his gloved hands over Lanné's chest, tracing the cage of his ribs through its padding of flesh. Another, a man with one eye covered by a patch, looked more closely at Lanné's face, stared deep into his two eyes. He held

Lanné's head in the span of his hand, prodded his cheeks and then pulled down his lower lip to look more closely at his teeth. Lanné thought to spit at him, but that too was beyond him.

The white-haired man blew on the scalpel and told the others to step back. The blade was lowered until it rested only an inch above Lanné's upper arm.

Not there, one man said.

Lanné felt himself tense.

Then where?

Chest.

No – abdomen.

The blade rose and Lanné relaxed.

The man with the eye patch said, His eye, and held up a small jar of liquid in readiness.

Ridiculous, someone else said.

The five men withdrew. The man with the scalpel held it rigidly upright. He stood to one side of the group, the blade pointed away from them, as though the breath of their argument might contaminate it.

Lanné remained silent, as he had remained throughout, straining to hear what was being said. The white-haired man saw what he was doing and pointed this out to the others. They stopped arguing for a moment and looked at him.

Amazing, one said.

He understands everything.

Might we not now have to revise our opinion of him?

A trick, the one-eyed man said.

The sallow-faced man approached Lanné and without warning slapped him twice across each cheek. Lanné felt nothing.

Nothing, the man said. He returned to the others and the argument resumed.

I've carried out fifty of these, the one-eyed man said.

None as important as this one.

And how many fatalities?

Forty-six, forty-seven, the one-eyed man said, but in a voice which suggested that this was no discouragement to him.

The white-haired man returned to Lanné.

You see what a problem you present us with, Mr Lanné. You see our dilemma.

It occurred to Lanné that the man was speaking to him as though he did not believe he, Lanné, could hear him.

What would you say if you could open your eyes, Mr Lanné, if you could hear us?

Lanné blinked hard, moved his eyes from side to side, but none of this registered on the face of the man standing above him.

Gentlemen, the white-haired man called out eventually, and the others returned to gather round him.

One of them came forward with an armful of other jars, larger than the one intended for his eye, each with its blank label, each half-filled with the same clear liquid. He arranged these in a line alongside Lanné's head, and to them he added an enamel bowl which rattled as he set it down.

Chest, the white-haired man said.

Two others said, Agreed.

A third said, If you insist.

The last, the man with the jars and the bowl, nodded reluctantly.

The point of the small blade was pushed into the soft flesh beneath Lanné's chin, immediately above his breast-bone. He felt it approach, felt the chill of the metal, and then nothing.

That's it, someone said.

Congratulations.

Hardly any blood. Surprising.

This will make your name.

This will make all our names.

The peering faces moved closer to him. He could feel their breath on his face.

The white-haired man paused for a moment. His eyes met Lanné's, but still there was no contact. He looked as though he were about to speak, to reassure Lanné or offer up a short prayer on his behalf. But instead he said only, Gentlemen – a word to draw them all back together and to focus their attention.

And then he drew the scalpel swiftly down the full length of Lanné's body.

Lanné gathered his strength to cry out.

The man with the bottles held one close to his face and wrote on the label. He asked if it was necessary to use the Latin spelling of the name, or if that wouldn't be going too far. A tension was released and someone laughed.

The dissection lasted an hour, and only after his every part and bone and muscle and organ had been revealed, examined and commented on, only when the cyclops came through the others and cupped both his hands around Lanné's beating heart and tried to wrench it from his chest, did Lanné finally scream out in pain and beg them to stop.

In an instant he pulled free of all his restraints and sat upright, alone in the darkness, kneading and pulling together the severed edges of his slippery flesh until the miracle was worked and he once again found himself whole.

It was a night for dreams.

James Fairfax woke from his own and kicked himself free of the sheets. He scooped water from a bowl and doused himself. It was a vivid dream, rooted in distant memory, its boundaries lost, details meshed, light draining to shadow, darkness brightening.

He had been at Ballarat only a few days, but knew already that he would not stay, that if he did then he would inherit more from his cruel saviour uncle than he wanted. Even then he had

125

seen the man wading through the shallows of lunacy and staring out at the hidden depths.

He had taken a horse and ridden north from the house. He
had studied maps and knew that in this direction alone would
a day's riding take him to the boundary of the judge's land. In
addition, it was the only direction the old man warned him
against taking. It was his intention to spend the night, perhaps
longer, in the open. He took a tent, which he did not use, food
and reading matter. The country was well watered. The judge
had suggested he be accompanied by someone who knew the
district, but he had refused. As he rode he wondered if he were
being followed.

There were no boundary markers in that expanse. He was
shown two peaks on a map, drawn and clinging like limpets to
the otherwise featureless surface of a boulder, a hundred miles
apart, one to lead him away, the other to guide him home. He
was not accustomed to such simple reassurance; he did not
possess so crude a faith.

Afterwards, a day away, his other maps failed him. The judge
had joked that when he became too scared to carry on all he had
to do was whisper the word 'home' in the horse's ear. Everyone
within hearing of this had laughed at him. You'll die a week
before the animal ever does, the judge had said.

He spent the night beside a shallow river. He could not find
it on the map he carried, and to have added it to the confusion
of other features – even to have named it – would have served
no real purpose: he would not return. He was lost, reassured
only – as he was meant to be – by the sun and the moon of the
two distant peaks.

He was woken at dawn by the call of a nearby bird. It was not
yet four o'clock. The fire beside him had died to a cone of white
ash. Then the bird called again and he knew immediately that
it was not a bird, but the voice of a child, a girl, he had heard.
His mount stood a short distance away. He had tethered it to a

stump, but now the halter trailed free. He waited. Dirt and grass stuck to his face and hair. The same voice: definitely a child's, this time accompanied by laughter. He made a sound to which he hoped the horse might respond, but other than glance in his direction, the animal continued grazing. He rolled from his bed. His rifle lay where he had tucked it. He rose and took his bearings. For a moment he could not remember which of the two peaks lay to the north of him. And then he orientated himself by the brighter half of the sky.

Unstrapping the rifle from its sheath he made his way cautiously towards the child's voice, dropping to the ground when he heard it again, suddenly much closer, and this time accompanied by others.

He followed the river. A low cliff on the near bank prevented him from crossing. He was in a country of ridges and steep valleys, fern and high grass in the bottoms, timber higher up. He was convinced that for the first time in his life he was walking – crawling – where no one had gone before him. Even the voices ahead did not disabuse him of the notion. He felt brave.

In his dream he had made that same short journey. Except in his dream he could not remember being convinced that the noises he heard were human. In his dream he crept closer to the sounds, covering the last few yards on his chest and stomach, and opened the grass ahead of him to see a dozen wild pigs rolling around in a mud wallow alongside the river. Except they had not been wild pigs – or even the strayed wild cattle that had been his second guess – but fifteen or twenty native girls, playing and splashing together in a small pool, its water turned to liquid mud by their actions. Some were only children of seven or eight, but most were older – twelve to fifteen he guessed – and several others were young women with full pointed breasts. Two of these older ones sat on the steep caked bank of the pool and looked over those in the water. Even seeing them, and hearing them as they called to each other in their wild game, he could still not be certain that these were people and not animals he was watching. There was nothing to choose between the thick liquid in which they paddled and splashed and the glossy sheen which covered their skin and plastered their hair; the colour and texture were the same, and with the exception of the two young women sitting apart, it was impossible for him to identify individual figures, so entangled and restless were the bodies and arms and legs in the mêlée. Only their eyes and mouths showed clean.

And then – if not in the reality of his memory, certainly in the half fiction of his dream – almost as though to compensate for his disbelief, he imagined that there were both women *and* animals in the pool – pigs, perhaps, or dogs. Dogs, he decided, because wherever these people went their dogs went with them. He watched, mesmerized, attracted and repulsed by what he saw, and by what he imagined was happening in the wallow. The native women on the Judge's land were all old and worn out. The few young ones came under the care of a supervisor – his first contact with the League – and all wore dresses and were forbidden to expose themselves. As he watched, a baby crawled blind and crying out of the crater of mud and was grabbed by one of its feet and dragged back in. Girls were squeezed up above the writhing mass and stood on the shoulders of those beneath before slipping back down to be submerged.

All this he was certain he had seen in his dream, and in his dream he had been startled by the sudden scream of one of the watchers on the bank, and he looked at her and saw that she was pointing directly at him. She yelled again to attract the attention of the others, and they quickly fell silent and turned to look where she pointed. He had been seen and he could not hide from them. He found himself paralysed, hoping by his immobility to become invisible. And whereas in reality he had merely watched as the naked girls and women had one by one climbed out of the pool and stretched on the banks and in the grass to let the mud dry on them exactly as wallowing animals did, in his dream he watched as they all climbed out together, scrambling over one another, pushing and pulling in their attempts to get to him. They came towards him in a single mass, a single fifteen-headed creature with flailing arms and thirty legs moving in unison like the legs of a giant spider. And still he was unable to move, to rise and run and mount and ride and save himself. He was unable even to shout and frighten them or to raise his rifle and fire it over their heads in warning. It was as though wherever he touched the earth he was held to it, and even as this creature pulled itself free of the clinging mud and came through the grass towards him he was unable to cry out. He heard it shrieking with delight at having discovered him, the same high-pitched squealing and grunting he had mistaken for animal noises and which now sounded more animal than human. He tried to close his eyes against the sight but was unable to. It was pointless to cover his face. And then just as the first of the filthy dripping hands reached out to grasp him a shot was fired and he woke, fighting them off and kicking at the sheets. And there stood his uncle, the judge, grinning broadly, a smoking rifle in the crook of his arm. Two of the older girls stood pressed against him, stroking him and responsive to his own fondling. His eyes never left his nephew on the bed, and only when his uncontainable grin exploded into laughter did he finally disappear into the reality into which the scientist himself had so suddenly woken. The two young women remained, staring without expression for a few moments longer, until they too faded and vanished, until he was left alone, confused, and struggling to distinguish between what he had seen and remembered, and what he had been deceived into believing he had wanted to see.

He wanted to shout the man's name, to curse him, to be sure.

Somewhere in the depths of the house a clock chimed the quarter hour: it was how he had grown accustomed to measuring his journeys into the weary days ahead.

8

L ANNÉ made his final visit to the barracks eight days later, surprised and intrigued by the summons.

Since his return from Coal River he had heard nothing from James Fairfax. Walter George Augustus too had nothing to tell. He, like a child denied, had turned his back on the man. He had instructed Mary Ann to walk on the other side of the street when passing Macdonald's house. All Lanné heard were the rumours in the bars. Then he met Cupid, from whom he learned that the Governor was to be recalled to England, along with his wife, but when he pressed him on James Fairfax, Cupid only said, 'Who cares?' He spoke as though the man had become some kind of threat to them all.

What Lanné heard in the bars was that James Fairfax's illness had tightened its grip on him, and that lately there were days when he was unable to leave his bed, days which he passed in a narcotic half-sleep, and days, increasing in number now that he had been suffering for so long, when he became delirious and when there was nothing Macdonald or the housekeeper could do to stop him from crying out in his sleep and holding unintelligible conversations with himself when awake.

Only the indignant Walpole continued to insist on his recovery.

It was to judge the man for himself that Lanné agreed to see him, half knowing that a note of cancellation might arrive at any hour, half knowing that the scientist himself would not attend.

He chose not to ask for one of Walter George Augustus' suits, and instead he wore only a cloth fastened round his waist and between his legs, secured by a belt from which hung several pouches and amulets given to him by Bonaparte. They were similar to the ones Bonaparte himself wore, and when Lanné inquired what purpose they served and where they had come from, Bonaparte told him not to ask. He guessed then that Bonaparte had taken them from the two doomed men who had no further use of them.

On the morning of the meeting he walked from the camp to the barracks, following the ridge of higher land which rose above the road, from where he could look out over the dying river and the unbounded distance beyond.

Fires now burned to the east, towards Richmond and Sorrel, and on the far bank the ground was charred black, the few thin trees still upright ready to fall at the threat of an axe. Faint breezes fanned the mounds of smouldering ashes back to life, and here and there over the blackened earth a sudden column of pale smoke revealed where this was happening. New shoots took quick advantage of the cleared land and starved cattle braved the warm earth in search of them.

There was talk of the fire spreading to the trees amid which he now sat, and of the barracks being cut off from the town.

Lanné looked down at the few men and carts passing along the track. Then he studied his hands and feet: his soles had grown hard during the previous months and no longer bled when he walked barefoot. His hands too were free of the blisters and the cracking which normally afflicted them. He had also lost weight in that time. His stomach no longer protruded so far beneath his chest and his genitals were no longer pushed back between his thighs by the weight of his belly. His arms and legs felt harder, as though the muscles had in some way responded to their probing and measurement.

He saw James Fairfax long before they were due to meet. He

rode Macdonald's horse, but exercised barely any control over the animal. He sat slumped in the saddle, the reins loose around the horn, and every few paces the horse either stopped or wandered from the path to forage. Only when the scientist hit it with his whip did the animal lift its head and continue. But even that small exertion drained the man of his strength.

When, after half an hour of this slow progress, the scientist was directly beneath him, Lanné heard him talking to himself. Only his feet in the stirrups kept him in the saddle. His bowed head rested on the animal's neck. He continued mumbling, long grey hairs from the horse's mane caught in his lips. Lanné wondered at the effort being made by the man to keep their appointment.

He watched until the horse reached the barrack gates, where it was met by someone from the guardhouse, before rising and continuing along the ridge to where it overlooked the compound.

He entered unseen, climbing a wall and prising loose an unsecured shutter. He did not want to be stopped and turned back because he was not properly dressed.

He finally encountered James Fairfax in the room in which their every other meeting had taken place. The plans and charts which the scientist had tacked to the walls had been removed and lay rolled on the desk. Cases of his equipment and other packages lay mounded beside the door. James Fairfax himself sat at the desk, his head cradled in his arms as though asleep.

Lanné dragged a chair across the room, scraping the bare floor so that the noise might alert him.

The scientist looked up, puzzled, disoriented. His face was slick with sweat. One of his eyes was discoloured and swollen and remained only half open.

Lanné waited for him to recover his senses.

'You were watching me,' James Fairfax said eventually. 'This morning. Me and my listless nag. You were up on the ridge. Am I correct?'

'It could have been anyone,' Lanné said.

'Might even have been the two murderers, eh? The president and the freak.'

'Perhaps.'

James Fairfax laughed, but even that was painful for him, and he pushed a knotted cloth into the side of his mouth. It was several minutes before he spoke again.

'Do you not agree, Lanné,' he said, 'that the true test of a man's faith might be determined only by the manner of his dying?'

'Only if he knows he is dying,' Lanné said, surprised by the speed and the confidence of his reply – as though it were something he had long considered – and also by the harshness of his words in front of this suffering man.

'Quite,' James Fairfax said. The word remained a call for silence, an evasion. 'Would you not agree also, and here I repeat only the thoughts of others, of philosophers and poets, that while there may be a degree of beauty to be found in every situation, there is a certain degree of horror present also, and that these two emotions cannot exist other than side by side?'

'Such as?' Lanné said, uncertain now of where he was being led.

'Such as a newborn baby, a fat healthy screaming baby. Is that not beauty itself to the mother and father, to the proud parents?'

'And the horror?'

'Knowing that this healthy kicking infant might die, of course. Knowing that its screams for air, for food, for milk now, might soon turn to screams of pain, of anguish, of knowing.'

'Plenty of dead babies in this place,' Lanné said.

The scientist slapped his palm on the desk. 'You can't play the ignorant savage with me, Lanné,' he said. 'Not now, not after all I've revealed, not after all I've shown to you.'

'No?' Lanné rose so that for the first time James Fairfax might see that he was almost naked.

'Am I intended to be shocked? What do you expect me to say? What? I know you mock me, all of you. I am not a monster, Lanné, I was never that.' But now he spoke in the cold and measured tone of a man who might, if thwarted, become one, spoke the same way Bone pointed his empty pistol at the heads of the young recruits on the parade ground.

Lanné sat back down.

'You disappoint me, Lanné.'

'You told me that the first time we met.'

'Did I? Surely not. Surely my professional eagerness, my youthful anticipation ...' He looked absently around him at the empty walls. 'Or perhaps I knew it would all come to this before I arrived.'

'Still time to make a name for yourself,' Lanné said. He took a small cigar from one of the pouches and lit it.

'A name? Here? What kind of a name would a man make for himself in this God-forsaken place?'

'No, not here. Where it matters to you – Sydney. And if not there, then back in London.'

'Ah, yes, London.' The scientist ran a hand across his face and left dust and sweat in smears across his cheeks and nose. 'And did it never occur to you that I might ask you to accompany me, to return with me to London?'

'As?'

'As my –'

'As your exhibit. A sideshow, perhaps.'

'Is that what you honestly think it would have come to? Do you truly believe I value you so little?' He was then silenced by a bout of coughing, after which he sat back limp in his chair. 'Perhaps,' he said.

'Why today?' Lanné said. 'Why here? I could just as easily have come to your lodgings.'

'I needed to collect my equipment.'

'Someone could have brought it to you.'

'Our dear sergeant and his idiot lackey, you mean? This is valuable, delicate equipment. These notes and observations are priceless. Apart from which, I wanted to show you –' He stopped abruptly, as though suddenly aware of something he had intended to keep hidden. 'No, nothing.'

'What?' Lanné said, knowing the man could not now refuse him.

'It serves no purpose.'

'Something to do with me? With your work here?'

James Fairfax conceded that there was no retreat. He handed Lanné a sheet of paper.

'What is it?'

'I have traced your family tree. See the structure of the plan. Compiled from everything you told me, and from interviews with those few others willing to help.'

'Walter George Augustus, you mean?'

'Among others. You all think too highly of him. A bladder filled with the air of pomp and ceremony and ignorance, inflated daily by his fat child of a wife.' He had said too much.

Lanné studied the sheet. He knew that the scientist was wrong.

'You made it very plain that you yourself had little idea of the people from whom you are descended. Look it over. If there are any errors ...'

This was why the scientist had been reluctant for him to see the chart: it was too perfect, the names and dates and interconnecting lines filling the paper in an unassailable battle plan. Fathers, mothers, brothers, sisters, each accorded a place within the overall structure, each a brick and a line of mortar in the wall through which Lanné alone was unable to see. Whatever corrections he made, they would serve no purpose. The painting was completed, waiting only to be framed, hung and admired.

Then he found his own name, alone, somewhere along an unmarked path. Distant cousins skirted the plain on either side of him, most dead or lost, none of them calling out to guide him. His mother and father hovered above him, and the empty promises and lost comforts that were once his brothers and sisters walked alongside him. He recognized a few names; others he had never heard of. Some of the names leaned propped against faint question marks; others stood underlined with dots, as though they too were on unsteady ground. Lanné's own name, boldly outlined, stood at the bottom of the chart like a warning over a patch of quicksand into which everything was shortly to be lost. They would all stumble blindly after him.

'I drew it up several days ago,' the scientist said. 'Is it accurate?'

Lanné knew that it was not, that families and tribes had been confused, that dates of birth and death were wrong, that they had never mattered in the first place. The simple expediency of linking names by drawing lines between them had created a structure and an order where none had ever existed, just as the lines drawn between the stars of the heavens created animals and gods in the night sky.

'Well?'

'As far as I can tell,' Lanné said.

James Fairfax almost laughed in his relief.

'I hardly ever knew any of these people in the first place.'

'Of course you didn't. That's the purpose of the chart, to bring them all back to you.'

Lanné agreed, because to disagree would be to deny history, to shake the foundations of belief itself.

'Order. Order in all things,' James Fairfax said. He took back the precious chart. 'I look upon this as my final achievement – if that is not too strong a word for it.'

'It *is* an achievement,' Lanné said, unwilling to enter any further into the deception and wondering at the limits of the scientist's own self-delusion.

'I value that,' James Fairfax said, and he quickly rolled the sheet and slid it into a card tube. Then he rose from his seat and leaned forward across the desk. 'You were never going to defeat me, Mr Lanné. You do realize that?'

At first Lanné refused to believe that the man was gloating, that his self-satisfaction had crossed this line into malicious smugness.

'Nothing would have changed,' Lanné said eventually. 'I'm still the last. Nothing's going to change that.'

'My point exactly. But without me you would have died unobserved and unremarked. We shared, you and I, something of that strange, one might almost say perverse, interdependence of the hunter and his prey. You do agree?'

'I'm not dead yet,' Lanné said, and unwilling to tolerate any more of this goading – which he ascribed as much to the man's illness as his misplaced sense of triumph – he rose and left him. Behind him, through the closed door, he heard the scientist's laughter, heard it follow him as he crossed the compound, walked out of the square and climbed again the loose, dry slope of the ridge.

The last of any pity he still felt for the man drained away an hour later.

He sat and watched the overloaded animal, watched it come closer and then stop beneath him, and watched the man who sat so loosely in its saddle turn, shield his eyes against the sun, and look directly up to where he sat. It was a gesture of defiance, unnecessary confirmation.

Lanné knew that he could not be seen, his body lost in the light and shade of the trees which surrounded him. He wondered what further move the man might make. His mount turned from side to side, swinging its neck and rattling its harness, but the man sat upright, his eyes fixed on where Lanné sat. His packages lay strapped around him; even a gentle trot would dislodge them.

He wondered what the scientist expected him to do. Did he wish to be confronted out here on this neutral ground? Did he think Lanné was in the company of the others – the murderers perhaps – and that all of them might now leave their cover and attack him? So immobile was Lanné that a lizard appeared from beneath a rock and moved ponderously over his feet. He could feel the testing flicker of its tongue, the rasp of its belly and tail.

Then a noise diverted his attention back to the road. A short distance away, along the bank of the river, a gang of soldiers and prisoners was clearing a firebreak, uprooting the dead scrub and burning off the last of the withered reeds to create a swathe of open land over which any fire would be unable to cross. One of these men had fired his pistol. The gunshot was followed by laughter, and by several of the men running away from where they stood. More laughter, then name calling. And then the long lifeless rope of a dead snake was thrown high into the air above them.

Lanné watched these distant figures, waiting until they and the dust around them settled after their excitement. It was close to noon and he guessed that they had finished work for the day. They came away from the riverbed in single file, wandering amid the uncleared scrub back to the road.

Looking down, he saw that the scientist was watching them too, and that his horse was no longer grazing, but now stood with its head back, stamping its forelegs and snorting. The gunshot had alarmed it. The scientist pulled in the slack of the reins, but to little effect.

Lanné rose from where he crouched, ready to run down and help.

And then he saw something else: two other figures, much closer than the scrub clearers, emerged from the trees immediately ahead of the scientist. He recognized the homesteader and his Gorgon-headed labourer. The farmer carried a rifle and held it ahead of him, pointing with it as he approached the horse. The other carried a club and a spear, and as he followed his employer he chanted and stamped his feet in a barely noticeable dance. It was the presence of these two, Lanné realized, and not the gunshot, that had frightened the horse. Even at that distance there was still something unsettling about the appearance of the man whose ragged braided hair made his head appear too large for his thin shoulders.

Lanné started to make his way down the slope.

At the sound of the second gunshot he threw himself against a tree to stop his descent. This time it was the homesteader who had fired. Alerted by the shot, the distant gang ran towards the scientist.

The man had discharged his weapon into the air close to the horse. The creature turned and half rose, and without warning the fieldhand knocked the homesteader to the ground and pulled the rifle from him.

Lanné resumed running down the slope.

As he approached the road he saw James Fairfax struggling to control his mount and then watched as he fell from the saddle and slid to the ground. Some of his precious packages were dislodged and these too fell and scattered around him. The homesteader and the native were now fighting over possession of the empty rifle as the first of the soldiers ran shouting towards them.

An instant before Lanné left the cover of the trees and came into the open, a third gunshot sounded and he heard the ball pass close by him, ripping through the foliage as it went. He dropped to the ground and waited, only looking up when no others followed it. It had come from one of the soldiers, fired as a warning over the fighting men.

He watched as James Fairfax rose unsteadily to his feet, holding his head and trying to understand what was happening all around him. The scientist looked down at his packages, some broken open, their contents spilled, and at the two men locked together at his feet, and he backed away from them. The first of the soldiers reached him, grabbed his arm and spun him round. Both Lanné and the scientist recognized Bone in the same instant. The others raced past them to the horse and the fighting men.

The homesteader was the first to pull himself free and struggle to his feet. On the ground the native still held the discharged rifle. He too attempted to stand, but one of the prisoners kicked him back down and another pulled the weapon from him and ran back to show it to Bone. The homesteader ran alongside him, collided with James Fairfax and then attempted to drag him back to where the native still lay on the ground. Each time the man now tried to rise someone else kicked his arm or leg from under him; others stood with their own weapons pointed down at him. Someone threw the dead snake at him, and when he tried to kick it away, thinking it was still alive, two others held him while a third fastened it around his neck. The man screamed and all those standing above him burst into laughter. Amid all this, Bone shouted questions at the man. He did nothing to stop the kicking and grew exasperated when the man was unable to answer him. The homesteader told everyone how he had saved the scientist's life. The man on the ground was accused of having stolen the rifle and then firing it at James Fairfax. This was what had caused him to fall from his horse.

Lanné overheard all this where he knelt hidden at the treeline. He waited for the scientist to dispute what the crazed homesteader said, but he said nothing. He was still supported by Bone, and looked close to collapse. The only voice now was that of the homesteader, who shouted and gesticulated at the man on the ground until his own inexplicable anger became uncontrollable and he resumed his kicking.

'Tell them,' Lanné whispered.

141

But still the scientist said nothing. Instead he came closer to the beaten man and simply pointed down at him. He seemed mesmerized by the figure on the ground.

It then occurred to Lanné that, in his confused and weakened state, James Fairfax might even think it was him, Lanné, in the dirt before him.

'Tell them.'

And believing he was about to be rescued by the truth, the man again tried to stand. He held out his hand to the scientist, but James Fairfax did not reciprocate. Instead he took a step back and pointed again, and at this signal the dozen or so others who had by then arrived at the scene joined in the attack, forming a circle around the man so that escape was impossible and so that every one of their kicks might find some soft target on his curled and defenceless body. His screams for help and for them to stop were drowned in their excited laughter, in their jubilant calls to each other and in the uncontainable grunting of their exertions.

Only Bone and the scientist did not participate in this savagery, but both watched it, and both encouraged it, and both, Lanné saw, swung their own legs in sympathetic gestures with the attackers.

After a few moments the man on the ground stopped screaming and trying to protect himself. His body lay as inert as a half-filled sack of grain, slack and unresisting to the blows which still came. The dead snake lay in pieces around his bloody head and chest, chequered tubes themselves covered in blood, flies already swarming to the meat.

A minute later the beating was over, and the soldiers and prisoners stood back, panting, grinning insanely and congratulating themselves on what they had done. Some turned to James Fairfax, expecting his thanks for being rescued and for the punishment they had meted out to his attacker.

And when all this was done, and when, for all Lanné knew,

the man on the ground might have been dead, he watched as
Bone and the scientist walked forward together to inspect the
body. Only then did James Fairfax begin to shake his head
and repeat the word 'No' over and over, as though only then
was he coming to his senses after his fall, and as though only
then did he fully understand the brutality of what had just
taken place and his own undeniable provocation and role in
it. He crouched down as though about to embrace the bat-
tered man, but Bone pulled him roughly back, telling two
others to drag the body off the road and into the trees. James
Fairfax made no effort to stop them. The two men kicked
aside his bags and cases as they pulled the body away. The
homesteader followed them, swinging the butt of his rifle
into the unconscious man's legs as they trailed loosely behind
him.

Lanné spent the rest of the day alone, trying to understand
what had happened, convinced now that the scientist had
known he was watching, and convinced too that he alone,
James Fairfax, had possessed the power and authority to pre-
vent the beating and that he had allowed it to continue for
some perverse and inexplicable reason of his own. Lanné had
seen what he would never have believed possible. The man
had turned away from him with a smile on his face and then
turned back and fixed him with the snarl of a dog. And if a
man were capable of standing back from such violence, then
he was equally capable of perpetrating it. The anonymity and
strange appearance of the victim had both played their part in
the tangle of motive and consequence.

Later, he told Eumarah what he had seen, and it was only
then, as he struggled for the words to frame the violence, that
he became convinced that the man was dead.

'Describe him to me,' Eumarah said.

143

He told her first about the man's hair and saw her catch her breath.

'And what happened to him afterwards?' she asked when he had finished, and as he sat with his face cradled in his hands, feeling the warm tears pool in his palms.

She knew the man, and her concern, he realized, was born of some distant, rooted intimacy rather than any immediate sense of outrage, and he wished he had guessed all this before his full and graphic account of the attack. But he knew also that he could not have left any of those details out of his account, that they needed to be spoken and be heard. He dreaded her asking him why he had not gone to the man's rescue, or at least why he had not gone to examine the body after all the others had left.

Throughout her questioning, Eumarah sat with her back to him, her hands clasped in her lap. He watched the tremor of her shoulders.

He lied to her. 'After all the others had gone, the home-steader's wife and daughters came out of their house, picked him up and carried him back there.' But it was not a lie, and as he spoke he saw the woman and the children with their load.

'She's a good woman,' Eumarah said, acceding to this deception.

'We could go and see her,' he suggested.

She shook her head.

In truth, the scrub clearers and the homesteader had parted company with the scientist and gone back to the barracks, where they spent the afternoon drinking in their bunks and elaborating on their own individual parts in the beating. James Fairfax had returned to town, leading his horse and accompanied by Bone, who had business there.

As he waited for Eumarah to say more, Lanné wished that either Ruby or Pearl would arrive to relieve him of the burden of her silence. He wanted the cold and undeniable facts of the matter to be embroidered upon; he wanted their guesses and speculation to wear down the edges of the truth, to penetrate its unthinkable spaces and slowly soften and break it down just as the sun and the cold turned the desert boulders to dust.

'His name is Daniel,' Eumarah said eventually. She signalled for him not to speak to her, not to ask her why she chose this name above his others. Then she rose and left him, and he heard her outside, calling to the dogs, and he heard her weeping, her loud and uncontrollable sobbing slowly drowned out as the animals ran barking towards her.

9

THE FOLLOWING morning he persuaded her to visit Walter George Augustus with him. They would explain what had happened and get him to use his influence via whatever committee might be able to investigate the incident or do something for the man.

But when they arrived, Mary Ann was alone. She greeted them from the veranda, where she lay on a chaise longue, her head in the shade of a giant leaf. She fanned herself. A small boy sat cross-legged on the ground beside her, a jug and glasses beside him.

She heard them approach and shielded her eyes to peer out into the bright light at them. She had been expecting someone else and was disappointed.

'Like Cleopatra,' Lanné whispered to Eumarah.

'My husband isn't at home to visitors,' she called down to them, as though this might stop and turn them.

'We'll wait,' Lanné called back. He recognized the boy with the jug and waved to him. 'Hot,' he said, and the boy took two glasses to them. Mary Ann contained her anger. She swung her legs to the ground and sat up, uncertain of how she might assume control of the situation.

'Can he fetch some more drink?' Lanné said. 'The jug's almost empty.'

Before Mary Ann could reply, the boy picked up the jug and ran into the house.

Then Mary Ann remembered. 'Actually, my husband was

called away on urgent business. Military involved. Police too, probably.' She paused, hoping the silence might add some measure of gravity to her revelation.

'Don't tell me – the scientist has been attacked.'

Mary Ann deflated. 'How did you know? Some savage came at him on the barracks road yesterday. Knocked him off his horse and tried to shoot him.'

Standing close beside Lanné, Eumarah only stared. Unlike him, she had prepared herself for this.

'Don't tell me,' Lanné said to Mary Ann. 'He was only saved because a gallant homesteader and party of brave soldiers came to his rescue.'

Mary Ann glared down at him.

The boy returned, carrying a full jug. Lanné helped himself. This time there was more spirit in the drink. The boy touched a finger to his lips as he handed it over. Lanné winked at him. This was where the argument would be won and lost. Eumarah covered her glass with her hand.

'Sorry,' Lanné whispered to her.

Mary Ann gestured for her own glass to be refilled.

'And I suppose the waddling great almighty Walter George Augustus is already fully appraised of all the facts.'

'What did you call him?' Mary Ann burped loudly and immediately covered her mouth. 'It's his business to know.' She stood blinking in the sun.

'And if he believes it, then you believe it.'

Eumarah tugged at his sleeve. 'Don't.'

'The man wants locking up and beating,' Mary Ann said, taking advantage of Eumarah's unwillingness to become involved. 'Probably got something to do with Bonaparte and that mob of murderers of his.' She emptied her glass and held it out again to be filled, satisfied that she had completed the circle of the argument and that she had won it. She drained the glass and smacked her lips.

No one had seen Bonaparte since Lanné had left him in the cave in the gorge, when he had risen from his dream of surgeons and gone out into the dawn. He was angry now that this connection was being made, and that it would later be repeated.

'Bonaparte had nothing to do with it.'

'How do you know? How does any of us know?' She was starting to slur her words. 'It won't be long before they catch the other two for killing that poor girl. And then it'll be his turn.'

'What do you mean?'

Mary Ann wasn't sure what she meant. The remark had been more irresistible blow than genuine accusation. But encouraged by her earlier victory she began to mould the words into something more specific.

'Everybody knows what he gets up to,' she said. 'He robs graves. He kills stock. He steals horses. So what if it wasn't him who attacked the scientist, he'll still have had a hand in it. He's a bad influence. He unsettles people. That's it – he's an unsettling influence. People do things just because he's around. They look at him and think they've got to prove something.' Again she was losing sight of her argument, but she was pleased that some more solid connection had been made. She waved her empty glass at the boy and then fell back on her cushions.

An impasse had been reached, and just as Lanné and Eumarah refused to leave, so Mary Ann refused to abandon the veranda and retreat into the security of her home. She wished her husband could see her battling in the breach of his absence.

But Walter George Augustus did not return for another hour, by which time the jug had been twice refilled. He came on a horse he had been loaned, a massive Clydesdale with a neck as solid as a trunk and a bolus of hair on each hoof. A harness of saliva hung from the animal's mouth and a froth of sweat flecked its chest. It was an entrance Walter George Augustus greatly enjoyed.

149

He dismounted and composed himself, straightening his collar and tugging at the hem of his jacket.

He saw first his wife, surprised that she was not indoors waiting for him. Then he saw the jug and the empty glasses. She called to him and waved. Then a movement at the edge of his land alerted him to the presence of the two others.

Mary Ann called out again, but in rising to greet him she stumbled and fell.

'You found the evil bastard who attacked the scientist?' Lanné said, coming towards him.

Watching his wife crawl across the boards of the veranda calling his name, Walter George Augustus abandoned the shield of indignation that was his usual first line of defence.

'We will,' he said. 'We know who he is.'

'It's a miracle that he managed to pick himself up off the road and get away.'

'What do you know about it?'

'Nothing,' Lanné said.

'They do, they do, they know everything,' Mary Ann called out. She arrived at the steps and pulled herself up by the handrail. She stood panting at the effort. She beckoned for the boy to help her, but instead he backed away from her.

'Is she unwell?' Walter George Augustus said.

No one answered him. If she would not leave them and remove her embarrassing shadow from the proceedings then he would ignore her; it would be the same thing.

'James Fairfax, you will be pleased to hear, is none the worse for his ordeal. He is still suffering from his illness, of course, but no further injury has been caused to him. They are searching for his attacker now. Corporal Bone has given the Governor a full account of the incident. He saw everything.'

'They want you to help the bastard,' Mary Ann called from the stairs. 'To help him.' She swayed where she stood. 'That's what they came for. That's what they came running to us for.

150

Laugh at us behind our backs and then come running to us when they want something done. Tell them to go, get rid of them.' Her shoes had come off somewhere on the veranda, and as she came down the steps her dress caught and ripped on the rail. She inspected the damage and laughed at it.

Walter George Augustus could only stare at her in disbelieving silence. He was lost and alone in a strange forest and she was a suddenly felled tree falling directly towards him where he stood. He felt chilled by her.

At the foot of the stairs she fell again, and this time she continued towards him on all fours, her dress rucked up around her waist so that the barrel of her stomach and the kegs of her thighs were exposed. She continued to laugh, and each time she moved her hanging breasts quivered at the impact.

'We ought to go,' Eumarah whispered to Lanné. She still held the full glass she had been given upon their arrival.

'What have I said?' Mary Ann shouted, seeing for the first time the way her husband was looking at her. 'What?' She clutched at the front of her dress and pulled at its tight lace collar as though she were trying to rip it off. 'What? Tell me. Tell me. You all think you're so ... so ... so –' She began to retch.

Walter George Augustus could not bring himself to take even a single step towards her. He had heard the swaying of that tree before and could not now save himself from its crushing fall to the forest floor, and he flinched as the first and outermost of its branches crashed to the ground all around him.

Almost as though Mary Ann had willed it into being, the news arrived that Washington and Albino Billy had been captured and were now in the gaol at Tunbridge awaiting trial. A judge was on his way from Launceston and the jury was in search of a tree from which to hang them.

They had been tracked to a pool on the Little Swan, sur-

151

rounded, and then seized during the night as they slept. Washington's head was shaved and painted completely white so that it looked like the skull beneath his flesh, and Albino Billy was naked except for the woman's underclothes he wore in tatters around his waist and arms, and which the men who seized him tore from him and tried to make him swallow.

The reports were unclear. Some said that three men had been captured. And some said that a third man had been seen with the two others as they were being tracked. All three were believed to have been sleeping on the banks of the pool when the hunters struck. But only two were caught and bound and dragged to Tunbridge, where they were first going to be shown to the father of the murdered girl, who was on his way from York at the court's expense to see them.

All this Lanné heard from Bone, whom he met outside the telegraph office. Bone the hero.

'Hang 'em for certain,' Bone said.

'How many?'

'What does it matter? Thing is, she's being avenged.' Saviour Bone.

The remark reassured Lanné. Bone knew Bonaparte and would have been happier still to see him already in chains for the crime.

Stalker followed Bone out of the office, folding a piece of paper and tucking it into his pocket as he came. His left hand was bandaged in a ball of stained lint.

'Like a pollarded elm,' Stalker said, holding out the soft club for Lanné to inspect.

'He lost two fingers,' Bone said. 'Hard to be a sergeant with only three fingers. Hard to salute all those officers, see.' He folded two of his own fingers into his hand and held up what remained.

'Perhaps they'll promote you,' Lanné said. 'Sergeant Bone, hero of the hour.' He wanted Bone to know what he knew, but could not tell him.

Stalker smiled at the remark.

'You're in all this somewhere,' Bone said to Lanné.

'They caught the two wild mob,' Stalker said. He tapped the information in his pocket.

'It wasn't Bonaparte,' Lanné said.

'Just the two of them this time.'

'And now they're going to waste good money on a trial,' Bone said.

There was nothing more Lanné wanted to hear.

He crossed the street and passed in front of the house in which James Fairfax lay sick. Then he followed a course along the vanished river until he was out again in wild country.

He sat down at a signpost which pointed its lying fingers into the emptiness all around. A shadow flickered on the ground close by, and tracing it upwards he saw a hawk hanging above him. The bird, realizing its mistake, drifted in a swoop to one side, where it folded its wings, spilled the wind and dropped in a barely controlled plummet to the ground. Lanné followed it, standing to watch as the bird struck its prey and was lost to him in a small explosion of dust.

James Fairfax never again visited the barracks.

For a week after his 'ordeal' he was confined to his bed, where his sickness continued its deep and energetic probing of both his vigour and his hope. He lost weight. He stopped praying. It caused him pain to even lift his arms and legs. Sores blossomed in his joints. The skin of his lips, tongue and mouth tore and bled. Thought and reason were lost to him in the quickening whirlpool of his delirium.

During the few daylight hours when he was free of pain and in some control of his senses he continued with his work. He sought out loose ends, unanswered questions, unrecorded dimensions, and tied these up as though they were those ribbons he so assiduously fastened around his papers – flimsy enough in themselves, but inviolate and final once secured.

And during that week he sent twice for William Charles Edward Albert Lanné, but Lanné refused to visit him.

Afterwards, on the few occasions when he was strong enough to leave his bed, he spent his days alone in his room, now and then sitting outside in the shade of the malaleucas, reading, and writing barely legible letters, swaddled in the heavy blankets the housekeeper insisted on draping over him. She knew as well as any of them how close to death he had come, and how the baton of responsibility for his suffering was now being passed from hand to hand among them all.

On the day the fire broke out in the stockyard and burned down eight houses and the carter's warehouse, he was found by Macdonald on the ground. He had fallen and knocked himself unconscious. There was blood in his ears and two of his ribs were fractured.

Another of the Sydney mails arrived and left without him.

Afterwards, when he could no longer control the trembling of his hands to write, he sat in his room and dictated letters to the clerks from the courthouse, and occasionally to Cupid, ordered there by the Governor to assess the situation. It was by then common knowledge that the Governor was leaving; elsewhere his orders went unobeyed. Cupid himself resented being sent on these death watches.

James Fairfax wrote to Mackenzie and other members of the Protection League. He wrote to his uncle, now in the Melbourne Asylum. And he wrote to Elizabeth Mary Victoria, his passions and desires chilled and shaped and read back to him until he no longer recognized himself. There was no other way.

He started leaving his plates of uneaten food on the dresser by the window to entice the birds in from the garden. One morning the housekeeper entered his room to find the plate mounded with fighting rats. Others raced across the floor beneath the bed. She screamed and woke him and he moved with ease and even some small pleasure from one nightmare into another.

When Lanné continued to refuse to visit him, he sent for Walter George Augustus and asked him to intervene. It offended Walter George Augustus to hear the man pleading like this, begging almost.

'I think he might have confused Lanné with a priest,' he said later to Mary Ann. It was the first time he had spoken to her in ten days. They both now avoided the company of others: a small sun had been eclipsed and never afterwards regained its full brilliance.

Eumarah told Lanné that he ought to visit the dying man. She felt sorry for him. It was unlucky for a man to die along an unfinished journey.

A comet was seen laying its trail of fire across the Eastern Ocean, visible for a full hour in the lacquer-clear night. It flew from north to south, faded and vanished as it passed over the ice down there. As ever, it was an omen. The drought would soon end. Better times were to come. And every man watching tried in some small way to attach himself to the passing star.

The Governor declared that the stockyards would not be rebuilt and there was a riot.

In the barracks, burning embers from a fire on the ridge drifted down on the powder store. Men stood ready with pails of sand. But then a point was passed, and even before some of them were able to climb down from the roof of the burning building, it exploded to nothing beneath them. Five were killed, and only two charred corpses retrieved. One of these was a man found on his hands and knees, blackened, featureless, still smouldering, and with his hands splayed on the ground ahead of him like a praying heathen about to rise and resume his incantation.

On his second unwilling errand from the scientist to Lanné,

155

Walter George Augustus said a strange thing. 'You ought to retrieve whatever papers he has,' he said, shielding his mouth, as though trying to pretend that the suggestion were not his, as though someone else might have made it and he was merely repeating it.

'Why?' Lanné had already made up his mind to see the man.

'To collect whatever remains,' Walter George Augustus said eventually.

'Why should *he* have it all, you mean? Why should *he* be the only one to benefit from all this?'

Walter George Augustus nodded.

But there was more than scattered paper. There were whole files, diagrams, Wooley's photographic plates, the casts of Lanné's feet and fingers, the maps of his body and his head, his family tree. His geography and history filled the room.

'Go,' Walter George Augustus urged him. 'Save yourself.'

There was no wind and no cloud. The night remained warm and airless. Smoke rose in ghostly columns, gathered and hung above him in a pall.

At the edge of the town he heard drunken voices, singing and laughter, and he made a detour along the riverbed, returning to his original path only when he reached the scientist's lodgings.

He stood in front of the house and studied it. None of its windows showed a light. He guessed it to be past two, nearer three. It had been his intention to go to the rear of the building and find an open window, but as he approached the front door he knew it would swing open at his push.

He was naked, his arms and legs circled white, his chest and face dotted with ochre, and with rings of scarlet around his eyes to give him vision in the darkness.

If he had not come here, then he would have gone instead to

Walter George Augustus', emptied the man's chests and ward-
robes and made a fire of everything they contained. The blaze
would stain the ground for ever, and when the embers were
cold he would have retrieved whatever remained of the buckles
and metal buttons and scattered them all around him in the
bush as though he were sowing seed corn. This would be the
new breed, and Walter George Augustus would be their king,
Mary Ann their queen, and their children would be neither
black nor white, but transparent.

The door swung silently open and he went in.

He knew that someone was paid to sit with the scientist
through the day, and that a nurse was hired to sit beside him
through the worst of his nights, wringing out and replacing the
flannel cloths packed around his neck and forehead. He knew
too that Macdonald's attention was now directed elsewhere,
that two of his long-awaited supply ships had anchored off-
shore and run up yellow flags.

The cholera had seeped from Oatlands into Cumberland and
Monmouth. A family of nine had all been discovered dead and
wasted as close as Glenorchy.

He passed along the dark corridor, looking from left to right
at all the faces hanging there: moonlit family portraits; old men
panning for their unfound fortunes, newborn babies reaching
out for the same; young girls identical in lace bonnets and
dresses, ribbons striping their pale faces; men and women
grown as heavy and as dull as the oxen they posed beside,
cherished possessions. Some natives, farm hands and servants
beside them, more possessions, bowler-hatted, holding para-
sols over more precious heads; some standing stiffly with trays
of drink. A man sitting on a mound of kangaroos and wild dogs,
his gun carrier holding up the severed head of the largest
specimen, the blur beneath his hands where blood dripped
unstanched.

The house was filled with the wooden ticking of a dozen

157

clocks, as though it too were cooling in the desert night. The open windows encouraged no draught. The strip of carpet felt warm beneath his feet.

He heard the scientist long before he entered his room and saw him: he coughed, he mumbled to himself in his fevered sleep, his shallow breathing was tortured.

Lanné slid into the room and closed the door behind him. Only a lace cloth laid out on the dresser rose and fell in response. He stood and listened. The sick man was talking to his fiancée back in England, sometimes whispering, sometimes drying in his urgency to tell her what he wanted to say before his lungs emptied. His fingers fretted on the sheets and his face and chest were slick with sweat.

Lanné moved closer to the bed. He rested his hands on the brass rail and felt it shake with the gentle motion of the man's convulsions. There were others asleep in the house, but he heard nothing of them.

The photograph of the woman still stood amid the bottles and jars of Walpole's worthless potions. Some of these had been knocked over and their spilled contents lay in viscous pools on the floor and on the bedside cabinet. They scented the rank air. The half-filled syringe still lay beside her face. She looked directly at Lanné, and Lanné returned her gaze. On a nearby chair a guttering candle cast disembodied shadows flickering around the room, over the face of the suffering man and over the glazed eyes of the watching woman.

He was thinner than Lanné had seen him before. His bruises had grown darker. Pus ran from one of his ears and soaked into his pillow. This, too, Lanné could detect amid the stale breath of other odours.

He left the bed and went to the desk, upon which papers lay scattered. Others lay on the floor and in untidy bundles on every surface. He unfastened the bindings of several folders, but other than open the covers and fan the pages through his fingers, he made no closer inspection of them. There was no need. His loss was now a matter of official record.

It was as he stood at the desk, the open window looking out over the dead garden to the dying river and hills beyond, that he sensed movement behind him.

He turned slowly.

James Fairfax was no longer flat on his back, but lay propped on his elbows. He was not looking at Lanné, but casting his eyes all around the room, floor, walls and ceiling, as though following the flight of some erratic insect. Dead moths, their wings and bodies singed, lay in a circle around the struggling candle.

Lanné froze where he stood, uncertain if he had been seen in the dim and shifting light.

And then James Fairfax spoke. 'I see you,' he said, but with his eyes fixed on the door. He pointed to the jacket which hung there. 'I do see you.' And then he fell back to his pillow, the air forced from his lungs at the impact.

Lanné let the papers he was holding slide from his fingers back to the desk.

'I do see you,' James Fairfax repeated, then shook his head from side to side as though trying to dislodge whoever it was he saw.

Lanné moved closer to him, into the band of cold moonlight which fell across the room from the window, which flowed to the closed door, and where, in the patterned white of his limbs, he acquired his own ghostly luminescence.

He waited. Silence. There was nothing to be gained by invading the agony of the man's dreams.

James Fairfax covered his eyes with both hands, and then, as though even this small effort had been too much for him, he resumed his murmuring and his painful gasping for air. The bed and thin mattress continued to shake at his exertions.

Lanné came closer, and reaching amid the medicines he lifted out the photograph of the unsmiling woman. He held her close to his face and looked at her, but saw only his own puzzled reflection staring back at him, and he knew that she too had her secrets from the man, that she too was not so ignorant of the future as James Fairfax had once suggested.

He took the picture with him when he went, passing back along the corridor of other watching faces, past the watching dead and the yet ungrown, and out through the open door between its pillars of wood scalloped and grooved to look like stone.

He walked along the centre of the road to where it became a track leading to the camp, and where its surface shone into the distance like a river flowing in the moonlight.

10

THE TWO murderers were hanged five minutes' walk from the back of the Tunbridge gaol. They were hanged from the limb of a massive iron tree which had washed downriver at the time of the flood, which had lodged fast against a sandbank and which had recently started to sprout new branches and leaves.

A crowd of two hundred gathered. Both men stood bruised and bloody as the nooses were slipped over their heads. Someone had hacked the swollen lump from the albino's leg and presented it to the hospital. Neither man spoke or cried out. A preacher read a short prayer for their souls and was booed and hissed. Then twenty-four honest white men grabbed hold of each rope and pulled the two black murderers heavenwards. Those watching were surprised by the speed at which they left the ground. The tug of war teams cheered. Washington died instantly, but the albino rose and fell – some said a malicious joke, a coil of slack in the rope – until he was barely half a foot from the ground, and they held him there for the next few minutes as he kicked and spun. When he too was dead, Washington's body was lowered to hang beside him. Then they were left to the heat and the crows and the leaping dogs for five days until they were cut down and carried off into the bush by some unknown hand.

James Adolarius Loftus Fairfax died a week after Lanné's visit without ever regaining his senses. By then, every finger pressed into his slack and enervated flesh drew its print of blood. His sleeping tears turned red. Only the *Mercury* printed an obituary.

Those who had known him went to pay their last respects to his washed corpse. The room was emptied of its medicines, damning failures, tracks brushed clear. Boys were hired to fan a draught of air along the corridor and out into the garden. All his belongings were packed into crates by Macdonald. The housekeeper changed the sheets on the bed and swept and polished until the room lost some of its mortuary odour.

Walter George Augustus went with his disgraced wife. Mary Ann waited outside while he went in alone. The housekeeper was told by Macdonald to offer her tea, but Mary Ann declined, and the two women fought a duel of barbed silence while they waited.

Alone with the corpse, Walter George Augustus could think of nothing to say. He had not attended church for the previous three Sundays and had resigned his post at the Sunday school. He was relieved to see that the man's eyes had been closed and weighted shut. He searched through the few papers and journals which had not already been packed by Macdonald, but found only a single sheet which related to Lanné, and this was disappointingly empty except for his name printed across its top and a diagram of his mouth showing which teeth were missing, which discoloured, which chipped, worn down and cracked. He folded this small and hid it in his wallet. It was something, a token, a solitary timber from the foundered wreck.

Emerging from the room, he motioned for Mary Ann to follow him. Then, pausing at the door and tapping his brow as though the thought had only just occurred to him, he asked the housekeeper what had become of the rest of the scientist's belongings. The woman did not know for certain. None had been returned on the mail boat. Some, she thought, had gone into storage with a holding company at the dock, some had

162

been sent to Government House at the request of Cupid, and some, she believed, had been taken back to the compound and the barracks.

The answer pleased him. Wrecked and scattered by a careless tide on an unfriendly shore. Soon there would be nothing of the man in the house. As far as the housekeeper knew, no one had written from Sydney, or from the wide world beyond, to lay any claim to the papers or his measuring devices.

Walter George Augustus returned home. His wife walked behind him like an obedient dog.

Eumarah, Ruby and Pearl waited until the couple had gone before stepping from the shadow in which they waited. They stood at the bottom of the garden, between the river and the house, gazed up at the room in which the corpse awaited its angels, and chanted their prayer for it, barely audible above the hum of the flies which filled the air around them. Then they fell silent, and after standing for several minutes longer with their heads bowed, the three old women turned and walked back into the shadow from which they had come.

Later that same night Walter George Augustus burned the diagram of Lanné's mouth, holding the sheet between his fingers until the flame burned him too. He dropped it, and the corner of white was consumed before it hit the ground. Then he crushed the crisp black pieces under his foot until they were no more than the dirt into which they disappeared. He heard Mary Ann calling to him, asking him if he was ready to eat. He ignored her, and instead he licked the taste of the flames from his fingers.

Lanné himself did not visit the corpse. The man he had seen a week earlier had been more dead than alive and he had finished with him then. He expressed only small regret at the death and declined the Governor's invitation to serve as one of the pall-bearers at the funeral.

163

On that day, when a group of only nine mourners gathered to watch the coffin of yellow Huron pine lowered and covered over, Bonaparte reappeared at Eumarah's to tell her and Lanné that he was leaving. And by the way he said it they knew that this time he was unlikely to return. His time had passed.

'Where to?' Eumarah asked him.

'Back to the Western Tier,' he said. 'They aren't too keen to come looking in those parts.' The Western Tier was a hell where men had to remake themselves in wood and stone to survive.

Later, when Lanné and Bonaparte were alone, Bonaparte told him where to find the bodies of Washington and Albino Billy. No one need ever disturb them again. There were no digging dogs or post-planters where they lay.

Later still, when the time came for Bonaparte to go, Lanné sensed that he had something more to say. The sun was setting and it would be dark within the hour.

'Is there something else?'

And as though waiting only to be prompted, Bonaparte handed him an obsidian pebble upon which was printed the small egg of a man's thumb. Lanné had seen others like it.

'Whose is it?'

'Belongs to a man called James Portsmouth Morrison. He gave it to me.' He paused to see what Lanné remembered of the man.

Lanné thought hard. 'A few years ago. You went on a bounty hunt after him.'

'Pretended to,' Bonaparte said, tracing the three initials in the dust at his feet.

'He killed a storekeeper.'

'In Baghdad. Jordan Valley.'

'You caught him,' Lanné said. 'Brought him back dead. Said at the time that he was one of the last of the Stoney Creek pure-breeds. What are you telling me?'

'He's not dead.'

'They brought back his body.'

'They brought back the body of a man who tried to kill me. Might have been Morrison's brother. Might have been trying to protect him. They were still living in a family. Shot him in the face. Home-cast bullets. He came at me with his club.'

'So Morrison's still alive,' Lanné said, struggling to understand more precisely what he was being told. 'He gave you this. And because he'd given it to you, you couldn't turn him over to the trackers.' He looked down at the hole in his palm, the white dab shining in the fading light. 'Is he still in hiding? Is that what you're telling me?'

Bonaparte nodded. 'With his wife. Another pure-breed.'

At this Lanné quickly folded his fingers round the stone. The secret of its potency had been revealed to him and might now be lost if he did not conceal and protect it.

'Living in a cave,' Bonaparte said. 'Like animals.'

Lanné could not bring himself to ask if it was the same cave in which the two of them had spent the night after their visit to Coal River. He could not ask him if that had been the true purpose of their journey.

Bonaparte picked up his sticks and the bag of his belongings.

Lanné could not even ask if James Portsmouth Morrison and his wife had any children. One child, two perhaps, a dozen, all of them living hidden and unsought, and all of them taught to fall silent at the click of James Portsmouth Morrison's tongue.

The revelation made him lightheaded.

Bonaparte watched him for a moment and then walked slowly away from him. He knew that Lanné would not survive in the world in which he survived. In the world in which he survived all men were made of wood and stone. He envied Lanné his ignorance; envied too his certainties because those certainties had not yet been tested, and because, like his belief in the pebble, they had not yet been stripped from Lanné as endlessly and as painfully as they had been stripped from him.

165

He imagined Lanné behind him, but he did not turn to acknowledge him or raise his hand as he went.

For his part, Lanné too neither called out nor waved. He knew how worn their bonds had grown over the previous months. And he knew too how easily these men of wood and stone disappeared and how rarely anything of them was ever afterwards discovered.

In the distance, beyond Bonaparte, the sinking sun touched the Derwent Caps and melted them to nothing in its furnace. Only later would they reappear – only later when the yellow dulled to red and when the wheel of stars rolled out again across the night sky.

It was a final parting, and only when it was over and too late did Lanné realize this.

Only much later, six years and four months later, and at another parting, did Lanné finally understand that this was how Bonaparte had meant it to be, that there had been no other way. And not once in the whole of that six years and four months did he fully understand the true nature of his own salvation or deliverance, and for the whole of that time he carried with him that small black part of this other lost man.

That night he watched the fire which still burned across the Pembroke Hills, plotting its intermittent progress through the darkness. It seemed to him like a line of battling men, fighting, wavering, and then regrouping and charging again against some invisible enemy. He even imagined he could hear the rattle of gunfire, the calling of orders and the screaming of the wounded and the dying amid the noise of the blaze. Glowing embers seeded the empty bush all around him, nothing now to stop the harvest of the flames.